LIVING WITH THE CONSEQUENCES

CHRISTINE FRIEND

Christine Friend

Acknowledgement

I would like to thank my son

Louis Hood

For drawing the front and back cover designs.

Chapter One

"What have I done? Oh no, what have I done?"

"Nurse, said the Sister how long has Mrs Compton been like this, she is extremely distressed surely you must have realised this?"
"I am sorry Sister, but she has been like this off and on since she was admitted from the Nursing Home on Saturday".
It was 10 past eight on Monday morning and Sister McDowell was doing her first ward round after having a weekend off.
Sister McDowell took the notes off the trolley and started to flick through so as to quickly get a picture of Mrs Evelyn Compton's background.
"I see she is one of us Nurse, except she specialised in bringing life into the world".
Nurse Brown shivered, she wasn't sure that she could ever get used to this unfeelingly way of speaking about patients.
"Yes Sister, she was a midwife for 25 years, then her and husband opened the Care Home which, after her Husband died she eventually became a resident of".

"Yes, I see that, her distress must be addressed she will be top of Dr Grey's patients today, he is very punctual, If he doesn't arrive by 8.30am then remind me I will put a call out. Right, next bed".

It was a busy ward on a Monday morning, new patients having been admitted over the weekend. It was known by older members of the community as a cottage hospital. It had been the dream of the local landowner back in the early 1900's, but as time had passed and two World wars had come and gone the hospital now consisted of eight wards. This all situated in the small town of Blakedon, nestling in the picturesque countryside of Sussex/Surrey borders.

It was May 1978 but Nurse Susannah Brown, who had now been a qualified Nurse for nine months and was on her first ward after completing her 3 years training. She felt that the callings out of Mrs Compton related to something not so recent, possibly something that had played on Midwife Comptons conscience for many years.

Sister McDowell was not in a good mood for the rest of the day. Dr Grey happened to be on a study day and his ward round was taken over by his colleague Dr Lucy Clements, a very efficient Doctor, but a woman, which never went down well with Sister. It was however decided that

Mrs Compton should be given a mild sedative
and then reviewed the following day.
Not only was it busy Monday morning but
Matron had decided to do one of her whirl wind
ward rounds. Matron and Sister McDowell went
back a long way but on this particular day
Matron was out to score a few points. A
bedpan had been left under a patient's bed
fortunately unused. Mrs Wells, a heart patient,
had received a magnificent bunch of red roses,
of which one had exploded and left it's petals
on her bedside cabinet and, Mrs Morris, on
paying too much attention to the roses,
managed to spill her cup of tea all over her
freshly made bed just as Matron was
approaching.

For the rest of the day Mrs Compton remained
calm and dozed intermittently. Her daughter
arrived for afternoon visiting and was greatly
relieved to see her Mother no longer agitated,
although when leaving her Mother, Susannah
saw her purposely head for Sister's office.
"Good afternoon Sister McDowell, I am Mrs
Compton's daughter,Veronica Cousins. I am
pleased to see my Mother in a much calmer
state".
"Yes Mrs Cousins, Dr Clements thought it
necessary for your Mother to be given a light
sedative and then her treatment to be reviewed
tomorrow by our own Dr Grey."

If Sister had thought that her commanding position was all that was needed she hadn't reckoned with the next statement.

"As I said I am pleased with seeing my Mother calmer but my question to you is why was this done today and not Saturday when she was admitted?"

Sister McDowell was momentarily lost for words, at which point Veronica Cousins turned and practically marched out of the ward. Nurse Susannah Brown had heard this short exchange of words and was hoping that she could remain invisible at the bedside of the patient facing the Sister's office, especially as she had been on duty over the weekend.

"Nurse Brown can you spare me a minute?" came the sharp voice from the office.

Susannah would have loved to have replied "No" but in her clear voice replied, "On my way Sister".

"I have just been confronted by Mrs Compton's daughter as to why she was left agitated over the weekend, I will re-read her notes but, have you any answers?"

Standing uncomfortably, Susannah explained that the Dr on call, a Locum from the Brighton General, thought it likely that she was suffering from a urinary tract infection and wanted a specimen sent to path lab before any prescribing. Sister Mc Dowell raised her eyebrows and Susannah made a hasty retreat, deciding that it was time to check the linen cupboard and sluice, and lay low. It was when she was unpacking the newly laundered bed linen that Mrs Compton's callings came into her head, "What have I done? Oh no, what have I done?"

After 30 minutes of making herself busy in the linen cupboard and then 10 minutes in the sluice she thought that she should show her face. On opening the door of the sluice she immediately bumped into Doris, the ward orderly.

"Wondered where you're been hiding, that's made my day hearing Sister being put in her place, met her match there".

"Doris, I think that's a bit hard on Sister McDowell, she really does have the patient's best interest at heart".

"I don't deny that she does but Mrs Cousins is a force not to tangle with".

Susannah looked surprised "do you know her then?"

"Well" as she heaved all 4ft 10inches of herself up, "my son and daughter in law had to use her services when they had that problem with their next door neighbour and their fence. It was her who got it all sorted and no messing".

"So she is a Solicitor?" Susannah asked.

"Yes she is and probably one of the best".

Susannah liked Doris, she was a hard worker but any worries about Mrs Compton she thought it best to keep to herself. Looking at her watch, Susannah realised there was only 10 minutes to the patients supper, and medications still needed to be given so, with a smile to Doris she made her way to the treatment room for the drug trolley.

Chapter Two

Susannah's shift finished and feeling tired she made her way back to the Nurses home. As it was a small hospital the nurses home comprised of 8 double bedrooms where two nurses shared, occasionally squeezing in a third bed on the first floor. The floor above had the same size rooms but these were kept only for Doctors on call, Matron, and Sisters, and they had the added luxury of two bathrooms. The ground floor comprised of two kitchen areas, two lounges and bathroom facilities for the junior staff lodging on the first floor. Originally, when the small cottage hospital had been built, the medical staff had accommodation on the second floor of the hospital which was in the attic. When in 1952 it was decided that the hospital needed to be enlarged, a separate building for staff quarters was built in the grounds. As a name had never been given to the hospital it was deemed fitting to be called the Queen Elizabeth Hospital after accession to the throne of the young Queen Elizabeth the second.

Susannah, after training in the large St.Thomas's hospital at Waterloo, had been determined to secure her first job in a small hospital with a completely different environment. She was a little nervous to find that she would be sharing but on meeting Angela who at 2 years older, bolder and with a confidence that she hadn't yet found, knew that they would complement each other and become instant friends.

On her return to the nurses' home after her day's work Susannah found Angela already in their room. As she walked in she was greeted with a

"Hi, how was your day?"

Susannah gave a shrug "not really sure, Sister's in a bad mood and really dislikes female Doctors. I feel a bit unsettled about one of our patients, a retired midwife actually".

"Look Suzy, my turn for supper, bacon and eggs ok? Then we will chat over a nice cup of tea".

Susannah smiled back, "sounds great, don't start it yet I fancy a nice hot bath first, hopefully while there is still some hot water".

Grabbing her towel, wash bag, jeans and t-shirt she made a dash for the stairs.

Susannah was relieved to find not only an empty bathroom but plenty of hot water.

Soaking in a bath of lavender oil which her Mother had recently sent her Susannah felt the day's tribulations melting away.

By time she was in the juniors' kitchen/dining room Angela was busy cooking and chatting to two colleagues that she had trained with in the much bigger teaching hospital in Brighton. Fiona and Jackie were paediatric, male surgical nurses. They had also finished their day shift but were now discussing the merits of a trip to the cinema in town with a bag of chips, versus trying to make a meal of the few bits of food they had left in their part of the communal fridge. Fiona, sitting on the draining board was voicing her opinion

"look, neither of us have anything decent to eat why don't we just quickly change, the bus into town will be along in 25 minutes and we can go and drool over Omar in Dr Zhivago".

Jackie was not so sure,

"Perhaps because I have already seen it twice, and I still don't think that if Julie Christie and Omar Sharif had a daughter she would look like Rita Tushingham, her features are to petite!" Fiona answered.

"I don't even know why you are looking at Rita Tushingham, I only have eyes for Omar".

With that Angela chipped in "Fi, he is old enough to be your Father".

With this all four girls fell about laughing. Angela buttering some bread turned around to face Susannah and now with a serious look on her face asked her about the retired midwife.

"Now Suzy, spill the beans, you really did look quite upset when you came in today".

"I know, we all know it's not unusual to see a patient in a distressed state but it was what she said and the haunted way in which she said it!"

All three girls were now focused on Susannah. Susannah realising that they were concerned for her, repeated what she had heard.

"What have I done? Oh no, what have I done?"

Fiona jumped down from the draining board and in her forthright way announced to her friends,

"Right I'm off to the flicks, are you coming Jackie? Sorry Susannah but I think you are just having a sensitive day and it probably means I've burnt the potatoes and ruined the saucepan".

Looking round at the other girls, Susannah wasn't so sure that they agreed with Fiona but Jackie was making her way to the door,

She turned back" looks like Omar again for me tonight, perhaps catch up when we get back, come on Fi get a move on, if we miss the bus I am not waiting for the next one!"

Fiona checked her watch, "Gosh where did that 10 minutes go? Yes a quick change, catch you later".

With that, Fiona and Jackie disappeared.

Angela placed their supper on the table and they both began to eat. After a while the silence started to feel a bit unnatural and Angela,

feeling sorry for her friend put her knife and
fork down,

"Don't take offence over Fi's comments you
know she is a Matron in the making and
everything to her is black and white. I can't
make any comment about your patient but I can
see that she has struck a cord and now you
have to think is there anything, and I mean
anything you can do about it?"

Susannah had now finished her supper, placed
her knife and fork neatly on her plate and
pushed the plate away.

"While I was relaxing in the bath I decided that I
have three courses of action".

This time Angela raised her eyebrows.
Susannah noticed

"I know you think this is all a bit exaggerated
but Mrs Compton was very distressed in a way I
have never seen before and yes I know my
experience is only of nine months but there is
just something very strange".

"Ok I am listening; go on, tell me your three
options".

"Well the first one is ignore the whole thing and
just give Mrs Compton the tender loving care
that we do in a day's work. Two, speak to her
or, three, speak to her daughter and tell her
what she has said".

Angela kindly looked at Suzy "have you seen her
daughter, has she been in to visit?"

"Yes, I have seen her but she did tear a strip off Sister today. After visiting she confronted Sister over why her Mother didn't have any medication prescribed until today. To be honest Sister didn't get a chance to answer and I am not very sure that she is someone you can approach".

"Well that's it then, I think you have answered your own dilemma. You can't go to the daughter unless you go to Sister first. My advice is to enjoy your two days off duty and then see how your patient is when you are back on duty. At the moment you don't even know what her diagnosis is. Look, let's not talk about it anymore until you are back on duty. You have been looking forward to using that sewing machine your parents dragged down here don't spoil it now. Right I am going to catch up on TV but best clear up first. I'll wipe up tonight, can't do better than that!"

Suzy had listened intently as she did respect Angela, as not only was she a little older and had more nursing experience but she was sensible and kind.

Susannah answered "I have got to learn to switch off otherwise the job will end up taking over. Two days now of dressmaking and with any luck a new dress will be hanging in my wardrobe by time I am back on the ward".

"Absolutely right, now the only decision tonight is BBC or ITV" replied Angela.

The two friends cleared away, made a fresh mug of tea and spent the rest of the evening in front of the TV.

Susannah's two days were successful and by the end of them hanging in her wardrobe was one new dress ready for any disco or party that the girls may go to. Thursday morning she was up early for a full day shift. Her uniform ready and waiting. A quick cup of tea, biscuit and out the door for a five minute walk to Bluebell ward. Susannah always enjoyed this short walk to work. She seemed to have spent her life in uniform; school, brownies, guides and Red Cross but her nurses uniform, the pink and white striped dress with frilled cuffs worn at the short sleeves, white cap, cape, black tights and shoes was the one she was most proud of.

Chapter Three

Arriving 10 minutes early for handover, she made her way to the kitchen to see if any of the day staff were enjoying a quick cuppa and a slice of toast.

"Hello dear, how was your time off?"

Doris, the ward orderly, had just finished a cup of tea and was clearing away the cup and saucer.

"Excellent Doris, one very classy halter neck dress is now hanging in my wardrobe. Actually it looks great and I could see Angela was impressed so I thought perhaps I could make her one for her birthday, what do you think?"

"Well, that's a lovely idea but wouldn't it work out quite expensive?"

"Not really, Angela is the same size as me so I can use the same pattern. It's only the cost of the fabric and actually Angela does like trousers so I could make her the halter neck jumpsuit which is also on the pattern, so it wouldn't be the same as mine".

Before Doris could answer, Sister McDowell popped her head around the kitchen door.

"Hand over in two minutes".

Doris winked at Susannah and both immediately left the kitchen and made their way to start their duties.

Susannah walked into the ward and had a quick glance over to see if Mrs Compton was still there, but a new face was looking back at her. Susannah turned round to see Sister McDowell watching from her office. Susannah swiftly turned and joined Sister, two more junior staff nurses and the Night Staff nurse who would be handing over. Taking notes, Susannah forgot momentarily about Mrs Compton until bed 12 was spoken about.

The Night staff nurse was speaking. "Mrs Compton has now moved to bed 12. She is making good progress on her antibiotics. Her blood pressure and temperature are normal, no more agitation and a diagnosis of a severe urinary tract infection. Dr Grey thinks that with this progress she will be transferred back to the residential care home on Saturday. Right, bed 13".

Susannah lost concentration as to the needs of the patient in bed 13. Mrs Compton was still there. She had decided if this was the case then she wouldn't refer to her ramblings after all, it wasn't her business. She was a nurse and that was what she was paid for not a busybody.

Hand over was complete, the night staff nurse left. Beds needed changing and patient's needed washing, all already for Dr Grey's ward round.

The morning flew by. One of the three new patients who had been admitted over Susannah's two days off decided to vomit just as Dr Grey reached her bed. Sister McDowell looked on very disapprovingly as though being ill in front of a Consultant wasn't acceptable. Susannah and Doris flew into action and in 20 minutes the guilty patient looked clean, tucked up in a pristine bed and actually looked better for her indiscretion.

At 11.30am Susannah was making sure the patients were ready for lunches and bed tables and cutlery were in place, when Mrs Compton called out to her.

"Nurse, Nurse Brown, have you got a minute dear?"

Susannah looked round,

"Yes of course Mrs Compton, I'll just fill this water jug then I will be with you". Susannah felt a sense of panic and was relieved that she had time to compose herself with the menial task of filling a water jug.

"Here I am Mrs Compton, what can I do for you?"

Mrs Compton lent forward in her bed and beckoned her closer. She wasn't smiling and looked pale.

"Dr Grey this morning said how pleased he was that my diagnosis was a UTI and that my agitation was due to that. I asked Sister if she knew what I had been saying but she indicated that you were the nurse on duty looking after me".

"That's right Mrs Compton I was, you were calling out and I could hear what you were saying but I am sure it wouldn't have meant anything so please don't worry".

The reaction Susannah had from this statement was not what she was expecting. Mrs Compton immediately became very annoyed.

"How dare you tell me not to worry, you know nothing about me!"

Susannah looking shocked and thought it best to have some privacy, so she pulled the screens around the bed. By time she was facing Mrs Compton, her anger had gone and she was quietly sobbing with tears rolling down her face, Susannah reached for her own cotton hankie and passed it to her patient.

For Susannah it seemed ages until her patient had composed herself but in reality it was only a couple of minutes.

"I am so sorry dear I don't know what came over me, I am just concerned that in my agitated state I may perhaps have spoken of a private matter".

Doris's voice could be heard further up the ward as she was handing out the lunches to the patients.

Susannah thought to carry on with this discussion now would cause too much notice so taking control she said,

" Mrs Compton I am going to open the screens and I will come back after lunch and you can ask me anything you want to, but please don't worry".

Sister Mc Dowell's voice could be heard above the rest of the noise on the ward.

"Nurse Brown, Nurse Brown".

Susannah opened the screens smiled at Mrs Compton, she then went to find out what Sister wanted her for.

"Nurse Brown, can you please go on your break now as I need you back for 12.45pm. Matron has just phoned, she would like to see me at 1pm to day".

"Yes, thank you Sister, I will go now".

That was a shame Susannah thought, she was planning to talk over her ordeal with Angela but she was on a later lunch break. The fact that Sister had to see Matron did mean that she would have a chance to sit with Mrs Compton with some privacy, hoping that the patients afternoon rest time was exactly that.

When Susannah appeared back on the ward Sister McDowell already had her cape on and smiled appreciatively at her as she was five minutes early.

"Thank you Nurse Brown for being so punctual, I knew I could rely on you. You have a mature

attitude towards your vocation which does you proud. There is no change with any of the patients while you were on your break. If you can just make sure that everyone rests this afternoon and keep an eye on beds 8 & 9, they appear to be old acquaintance's and I don't want to move them as they seem in a good way to be pushing each other's recovery along but you know how I feel about the rest time".
"Yes Sister, no problem".
 With this, Susannah glanced up at the ward clock and Sister McDowell saw her look and realised time was ticking by, she wrapped her cape around her and was off to her meeting with Matron.
Taking on Sister's compliment, for which she was known not to give very often, Susannah did a perfunctory walk around the ward having a quick word with every patient, really just to ensure that when she sat with Mrs Compton they wouldn't be disturbed. After one vase of flowers was taken and refilled and one of their regular patients, Mrs Bench had yet again lost her glasses (Which were found tucked under her pillow) Susannah turned the ward lights down and waited to hear the gentle breathing and slight snoring noise of 14 out of 15 patients. Very quietly she pulled the screens around Mrs Compton's bed. Her patient was sitting upright, quite clearly looking unsettled. Susannah noticed that her hankie which she had given her

before lunch was being rigorously twisted around her fingers.

Susannah moved a chair much nearer to the bed and placed her fingers over her lips so that Mrs Compton was aware that they would almost be whispering to each other. Not only was this not to wake any patients but Susannah didn't want any one else to hear what was going on.

Susannah thought it best if she spoke first.

"Mrs Compton you were calling out but I am sure I was the only person to hear it".

"My dear can you recall what I said?"

"Yes it was, 'What have I done? Oh dear, what have I done?' Mrs Compton I don't think you should explain yourself to me but it seems that you need to speak to someone".

"I've been laying here now thinking the same but I have done something very serious, probably criminal, and I know it can't be put right."

Susannah noticed that her hankie was beginning to look ragged as the twisting was intensifying, thinking if this little chat goes badly she could either be facing Sister or even Matron.

"Look, if you think it could possibly be criminal then why don't you speak with your daughter".

Her deep blue eyes looked up at Susannah "because we don't and never ever had that kind of relationship. I love my daughter dearly but

Veronica has always been,' shall we say, forth right' even as a child".

Susannah was feeling totally out of her depth. "Mrs Compton, it wouldn't be professional for me to allow you to confide in me, and your daughter does visit every day so you will be seeing her sometime today. You say she is, forgive me for saying 'forthright' well, then her professional advice will be practical and not emotional".

With this advice Susannah stood and looking at Mrs Compton realised that she had struck a note, and Mrs Compton looking at Susannah realised that the advice she had just been given was the only answer.

Chapter Four

Afternoon rest on Bluebell ward was over at
2.30pm. That gave the ward staff 30 minutes
before afternoon visiting. The lights came up
and Doris started calling out to the bed bound
patients asking if anyone required a bed pan.
 Sister McDowell arrived back on the ward just
as Doris's voice rang around the ward. Sister did
one of her disapproving tuts, turned, walked
into her office and closed the door with a
decisive bang.
At 3pm the ward doors were opened and the
rush of visitors came in. Evelyn Compton was
facing the doors raising herself up on her hands
to see if her daughter was one of them. After a
few minutes she lowered herself back on to her
mattress knowing that if Veronica wasn't one of
the first visitors in then she was busy and would
be in to visit in the evening. Looking down at
Nurse Brown's hankie she was unaware that her
son -in- law Edward was approaching her bed.
"Good afternoon Mother in law, how are you?"
Evelyn looked up to see Edward her warm,
smiley, hen pecked son in law.
"What a lovely surprise to see you Edward".

Then immediately feeling concerned as Edward only ever visited in the evening wondered if there was some kind of domestic problem.

Leaning forward to give Evelyn a peck on the cheek, Edward was smiling down at her.

"No problem, well you know nothing out of the ordinary. Veronica's tied up in court and she thought the case would be over before lunch but it has taken a turn and she really wanted you to have your clean nighties etc".

Putting a canvas bag on the bed, he heard Evelyn sigh with relief.

"I must say Evelyn you look quite tired, are you really ok? Veronica said yesterday evening after seeing you in the afternoon how much better you looked".

Evelyn smiled back at her very much liked Son in Law. "I am fine really, it's just I have been laying here and thinking about, you know, life and well, I think it's time for me to have a heart to heart with Veronica. Don't look so worried, it is old business relating back to my midwifery days. Nothing related to the family".

Reaching over to touch his hand. "Nothing for anyone to worry about. It's more professional advice; anyway that's enough about me. Shouldn't you be out on the golf course today, the second Thursday in the month".

Edward was now sitting and feeling more comfortable with the conversation once on the subject of golf he could talk for ages.

Evelyn and Edward sat and chatted until Doris
appeared on the ward with the tea trolley.
"Mrs Compton, a nice cup of tea, and would
your visitor like one as well"?
Evelyn felt very relaxed now she was enjoying
her afternoon visitor and it gave her breathing
space until the evening, when she knew that
her daughter who was never late would almost
certainly be the first visitor in the ward.
"Yes please, two cups of your finest brew please
Doris".

Chapter Five

Susannah kept a watchful eye on Evelyn
Compton for the rest of her shift. She was
responding well to her antibiotic treatment. Her
blood pressure and temperature had remained
normal after their little chat. Susannah guessed
that her daughter would be visiting later so,
providing the patient remained as calm as she
was now Susannah felt her involvement in
Midwife Evelyn Compton's life was over.
Promptly at 7pm Bluebell ward doors opened
and it was no surprise to Evelyn that Veronica
was first over the threshold.
"Hello Mother, what is it that you need to speak
to me professionally about"? While giving her
Mother a perfunctory kiss on the cheek.
"Veronica please do not harass me".
 By now Veronica had grabbed the visitors chair
and pulled it as close to the bed and her Mother
as it was as possible to get.
" I did say to Edward I wanted to speak with you
regarding something that had once happened
and I might add many years ago, but certainly
not here or now.Perhaps it would be better
when I am back in my own surroundings".

Veronica looked very perplexed it wasn't what she was hoping to hear. In her professional life she always worked on the principle to come straight to the point, that way the client was taken off guard and usually told you more then they were expecting to say.

Mother and daughter both looked at each other, neither of them feeling particularly pleased with the visit.

Veronica still feeling a little embittered by her Mother's words thought that she should show some compassion and with this thought, made her Mother an offer.

"Mother, instead of you going straight back to the home why don't you come and stay with us for a few days. A kind of convalescence. We will look after you and when we are both relaxed and the time is right we will talk. That way we won't be disturbed and there won't be any time constraint either".

Evelyn Compton looked again at her daughter and not only did she feel a Mother's love for her but she also felt compassion because she knew that Veronica had never shown any tendencies of loving care. As her Mother she had always thought she should have been born a son.

She now smiled and took hold of Veronica's left hand that was resting on the bed.

"That would be lovely but wouldn't it be hard to manage, surely you are not due for any annual leave at the moment"?

Veronica was quick to realise that her Mother probably didn't want to stay with them but was showing a huge compromise and it would take some juggling but in a cheerful voice.
" Please don't worry, after all these years of hard work there must be some benefits of being a senior partner".
Mother and daughter left it there and carried on the visit with more general topics such as the weather, Edward's new expensive set of golf clubs and what was in bloom in Veronica's garden.

At 7.45pm on the dot, Sister McDowell came out of her office and rang her little bell to indicate to the visitors on the ward that time was up. Her expectations were that each visitor would place the chair back where it was found a quick peck on the cheek or shake of the hand and be on their way. She wasn't to be disappointed within 5 minutes the ward have been vacated of strangers and her staff could carry on with their duties before handover and the night staff would take over.

Evelyn was pleased to hear the bell ring; she had a lot of thinking to do. Veronica bent to give her Mother a kiss, put her chair back against the wall and with a little wave disappeared with rest of the visitors.

The evening ward orderly had already started her first task by pushing the hot drinks trolley from bed to bed.

"Good evening Mrs Compton what can I get you tonight? I must say you are looking so much better. On the trolley tonight we have the usual; tea and coffee, but I also have not only Horlicks but hot chocolate as well!"

Evelyn would have enjoyed the luxuries of Horlicks or hot chocolate but her head was buzzing and she wanted to get things straight so she plumped for a very sweet cup of tea.

At 9pm the ward was quiet and calm. The lights had already been turned down to low and there was the gentle hum of sleeping patients.

In bed 12 the patient was very much awake. Evelyn wasn't consumed with the task ahead and her (owning up to her one and only monumental mistake) but instead she thought of her two beloved children. Her eldest, a daughter now 45years old, was a very successful solicitor, an extremely well organised wife and Mother, but at times no softness to her nature or sense of humour. Married to Edward, a Chartered Accountant, who seemed to run his business with calm, where as her younger child a son who at 43 showed so much compassion and care that in his chosen profession of Paediatrician, he suffered with his inability at times to be unable to cut himself off from his work. She then thought about her daughter in law who was able to cope with Michael's stress, running a home, two darling little girls and working part time as well. Evelyn's only regret was that they lived so far away. Evelyn always thought that one day Michael and Jenny would make their life in Jenny's home country of Australia. Jenny, working as a nurse at the Royal London hospital and falling in love with her clever son, would want her babies to have the same type of childhood that she had had. They kept their promise and had come back every three years for a 3 week vacation but it never seemed long enough and before long they were packing their suitcases ready for the journey home. Only when Gerald died, her husband of 35 Years, and Michael flew back to England immediately, did she truly realise how lucky she was. He managed to stay for four weeks with the support of his colleagues and many long distance calls to and from Australia. Even when she was first admitted into hospital and Veronica called him, he was prepared to fly home. This brought tears to her eyes. Not long after her reminisces of her children, Evelyn fell asleep.

Chapter Six

Saturday morning at 8.30am Locum Dr Lee was back on duty on Bluebell ward. Sister McDowell rose from her chair as Dr Lee walked into the Sister's office with an out stretched hand ready to introduce himself to the formidable Sister.

"Good morning Sister Mc Dowell, I am Dr Lee, your locum and on call Doctor for the weekend. I didn't have the pleasure of meeting you last weekend but I do hope everything was as it should be on Monday morning".

Sister McDowell in her long service was unsure as to whether this young Doctor was being sincere or not but decided that she would play along.

"Everything was fine Dr Lee thank you for asking. Now, if you would like we can start on your medical round. There are number of patients who could be discharged today but do need to have TTA's (Drugs to take away) and pharmacy closes today at 12pm so we do have to be prompt".

"Of course Sister, please lead the way".

By time they reached bed 12 Evelyn Compton was sitting up, hands resting in her lap waiting their arrival.

Dr Lee immediately recognised Evelyn as the patient who had been distressed the previous Saturday.

"Hello Mrs Compton, and how are you today. I have to say you do look much better than when I first saw you last weekend".

"Yes I am feeling much better and was wondering when I could be discharged. My daughter wants to look after me for a short while before I return to my residential home. So if it is a case of looking for any empty beds then please look no further".

Dr Lee smiled "that all sounds excellent to me, what do think Sister McDowell?"

"Mrs Compton you are making a very good recovery from your infection and I am sure a change of scenery for a few days will do you good. If Doctor would be so good to write you up TTA's for your antibiotics, then I will ring your daughter and give her the good news".

Evelyn smiled sweetly and Dr Lee and Sister Mc Dowell moved on to the next bed.

Doctor Lee was very efficient and methodical and quite quickly the ward round was finished. In fact Sister Mc Dowell was beginning to wish that he was not just their locum for the weekend as she couldn't remember the last time a ward round had been carried out so efficiently. Dr Lee sat at the corner desk to start writing up notes and TTA's. Meanwhile Sister McDowell reached for the telephone to start notifying her patients relatives of their impending discharge. Normally the organised Sister would start to make her calls in bed order but after the confrontation she had with Evelyn Compton's daughter she thought it best to make this her first call.

"Good morning, this is Sister McDowell calling from Bluebell ward regarding Mrs Compton may I speak with Mrs Cousins?"

A man's cheery voice replied "Hello there, I am afraid my wife is out at the moment can I take a message or even be of some help".

Sister Mc Dowell was taken aback, she had seen Veronica Cousins husband from a distance but was surprised to find how friendly he sounded.

"Yes if you would please tell her that her Mother is to be discharged this morning but is waiting for her medication to come to us from Pharmacy, therefore once it arrives on the ward a member of staff will ring you and you can make your way here to pick her up. I hope that will all be satisfactory? Now have you understood my message or would it be better if I was just to ring back a little later?"

Edward was smiling to himself, this was not the first time he had this kind of treatment with someone leaving a message for his wife. Had Veronica not already told him about her conversation with the Sister then he would have assumed correctly that they had indeed already met.

"No problem Sister, I will inform my wife of the good news as soon as she walks through the door which I would estimate will be in about half and hour, good bye and thank you again for the call".

Sister put the phone down and was wondering how Mrs Compton's son in law could be so positive about his wife's return. What she didn't know was, like with everything else, Veronica Cousins was just as organised in her private life as her professional life and Saturday morning was a regular appointment with her hairdresser. Today everything on Bluebell ward was running like a well oiled machine and the TTA's arrived on the ward for 11am much to the surprise of Sister. Doris happened to be in the Sister's office when the messenger arrived with the medication.

"Thank you Maud", said Sister "how nice to get everything back so quickly".

Maud, not one to hold back, "As I have said before Sister, if you get the treatment charts down early and don't sit on them up here then you will get the medication back quickly. Mind you it does help having that nice Locum up here. By all accounts he is a very quick worker". With a wink to Doris, Maud swiftly turned her messengers trolley and was gone out of the office.

Edward's estimated time was nearly spot on in fact Veronica arrived back 25 minutes later, and true to his word he imparted the good news to his wife as soon as she was through the front door. Veronica was pleased as she knew that her Mother was beginning to feel a little impatient still being in Hospital but she herself had this underlying feeling of dread that she had never experienced before. This was all due to the conversation her Mother was planning to have with her. She had tried to put it to the back of her mind because knowing her Mother, unless it was a serious problem she was extremely capable and over time would have undoubtedly sorted it out herself so, what could it all be about?

Edward put the coffee percolator on while Veronica got the coffee cups out. He could see his wife looked a little distracted and gently asked "Dear are you ok, a penny for your thoughts".

She placed the cups down on the breakfast bar and looked up at him. It was these moments that she knew how much she truly loved him. "Yes I'm fine, well actually I can't stop thinking about this conversation my Mother wants to have with me. It's so out of character for her to ask my advice on anything. Even when she decided to move into the Willows and told us both, it wasn't for our opinion, she had already made her decision".

Edward realised that Veronica who seemed to take everything in her stride no matter what was thrown at her was indeed concerned. He moved next to and put his arms around her. "You know it doesn't matter, whatever it is I will do anything I can to help. If it is something totally private then I will do anything I can to support you to enable you to help Your Mother. Please don't worry yet, as it is you don't even know if it is something to worry about".

She was about to answer when he bent and gently kissed her on the lips and just as he did this the telephone started to ring.

It was agreed between Bluebell ward and Veronica that Mrs Compton would be collected at noon. This would give Veronica enough time to pack the clothes that she had of her Mother's which had been laundered. These were the clothes that her Mother had been wearing when she was admitted into hospital. Then on her journey there, she would stop at the sweet shop in the Main Street of the small town of Blakedon to buy the nursing staff chocolates to say thank you for the care her Mother had been given.

At 12:00 on the dot Veronica walked on to Bluebell ward and knocked on the Sister's door. Sister answered without looking up.
"Come in".

"Hello Sister Mc Dowell, I have my Mother's clothes shall I leave them with you?"
Sister McDowell immediately got up, "Come with me and we will see what your Mother would like to do".
Both ladies walked down the ward to bed 12. It didn't take long for Evelyn to get dressed, and apply a little lipstick and face powder from her treasured compact that her husband had given her on their first wedding anniversary. She clicked her handbag together and spoke to her daughter who was on the other side of the bed.
"I am ready Veronica, have you packed everything and checked there is nothing left in the locker?"
"Nothing left in the locker Mother, all I need to do now is close the case and for you to hand this box of chocolates to Sister McDowell and then we are off".
Mother and daughter smiled at each other both relieved that this day had come and that the agitated state that Evelyn had been in on admission was no more than a symptom and not a condition.
Sister McDowell graciously took the chocolates from Mrs Compton and in return gave her a small white paper bag with medication in it.
There were handshakes all round and thanks from the now discharged patient.
No sooner had they got in the car then Veronica was already trying to organise her Mother. If

she was going to stay with her daughter then perhaps more clothes and personal effects would be needed.

"So Mother, what would you like to do, go to The Willows now or perhaps after lunch? Then later this afternoon we can get you unpacked and settled in".

Evelyn glanced sideways at her daughter, she didn't want to sound ungrateful but she needed to take her time even in going to her own home. She was well aware that in a few days time her relationship with her daughter could dramatically change. Evelyn felt that until they sat and talked she wanted everything to be done literally in slow motion.

"Veronica, what I would dearly love is a nice hot cup of coffee in your lovely kitchen, then, perhaps this afternoon, to put my feet up in the lounge. I was hoping that we could go to The Willows tomorrow morning to collect my things necessary for my stay. It's just I feel a bit tired and as much as I think Yvonne Kelly is a very good manager, she does so fuss and if we go tomorrow it will be her day off".

Veronica squeezed her Mother's hand. "Fully understand, tomorrow it is. But now, let's get home and see about that cup of coffee".

Twenty five minutes later Evelyn was sitting very comfortable on a two seater chintzy sofa in Veronica's extremely large kitchen. She looked around in wonder that such a large room could give out such a feeling of cosiness. When initially her daughter and son in law had bought this detached five bedroom 1920's house known as the Chimneys, Evelyn thought they were making a grave mistake. It had become very dated and unloved. Then to hear that they were going to open up the kitchen by knocking through a large pantry, dining room and the original laundry room and make it ' Open plan', apparently they had seen this concept at the Ideal Home Exhibition. She couldn't see how it was going to feel like the hub of the home but it did just that. Even with her two Grandsons away at school it didn't feel empty.

Next morning Evelyn awoke to see her Son in Law standing at the bottom of her bed with a cup and saucer in his hand.
"Good morning Evelyn, it is a lovely bright and dry Sunday morning. It's 7.15am, hope I haven't woken you too early but it's my turn to make the tea and I am off for a game of golf in 10 minutes".
Evelyn shook herself awake. "What a lovely nights sleep I have had. No not too early for me and a biscuit with my tea as well. I do feel spoiled".
Edward placed the cup and saucer on the bedside cabinet. His own Mother had sadly passed away five years before so to do

something as simple as making a cup of tea for his Mother in law was a pleasure.

"I am pleased if you feel you are being spoiled it means we are getting your stay here right. See you later I'll be back for lunch, roast beef today".

For Evelyn, the rest of day became a very traditional Sunday. Not long after Edward left for his game of golf Veronica knocked on her Mother's bedroom door.

"Good morning Mother, how do you feel today? I hope you slept ok".

Evelyn replied in a chirpy voice. "Like a log thank you. Now you mustn't let me get in your way. I am grateful and pleased that we are going to spend time together this week after you taking some of your well deserved annual leave, so if you have made plans already for today then please don't let me get in the way of them".

"That's very considerate of you but I have cleared my day for you. Would you like to go to Church this morning? The only time we ever get to go to Church together is at Christmas, and then after, back home for roast beef and apple pie, or we could go to the Willows instead this morning but it is entirely up to you".

"As much as I would like to go to Church with you I don't think going to The Willows can be delayed any longer. A few changes of clothes would be nice and I do have a much more comfortable pair of slippers there".

Veronica agreed that it was best for them to visit Evelyn's home and collect clothes and essential items that would make Evelyn's stay more comfortable.

The rest of the day followed the pattern that had been agreed. After both had washed and dressed Veronica made porridge, tea and toast. It was then into Veronica's car for the 10 minute journey to The Willows.

The visit took longer than both ladies had anticipated as almost all the residents wanted to say they had missed Evelyn and that they were glad to see her looking so well and how much they were looking forward to having her back after her convalescence at Veronica's. One and half hours later they were back in the car on their way back to The Chimneys.

When Evelyn was tucked up in bed that evening she couldn't believe a day could go so fast. A lovely Sunday Roast followed by a rest in the afternoon. Veronica was a very good cook and for tea they tucked into macaroni cheese followed by chocolate cake. Evelyn patted her stomach at this rate she would start to put on the pounds. She had always been proud of being able to keep her naturally slim figure but with the large portions that Veronica served her clothes would soon start feeling tight. No longer as active as she had been in her professional life, she certainly didn't want to let herself go.

Chapter Seven

Monday morning, Veronica and Edward rose early, showered and dressed. Veronica was down in her kitchen filling her coffee percolator when Edward joined her.

Edward looked around with a cheeky grin.

"Where is your Mother, letting her having a lay in?"

"No, I just thought, leave her to 8am then I will take her up a cup of tea. While I have been down here it has started to play on my mind about the chat she wants to have with me and strangely enough I am beginning to feel a bit nervous, so I thought if you had breakfast and then left for the office, I would then be in the house on my own and we might be able to settle and get this little talk out of the way. After all it can't be anything huge, Mother has always been a pillar of society and we know it can't be about money. Daddy left her so financially safe". Veronica shrugged and looked at her husband for support.

"Totally agree with you my dear. I'm sure she is worrying over nothing. As soon as I have eaten I'll be off then the sooner you have this chat the better for both of you".

Thirty minutes later Veronica was waving Edward off at the front door. She watched him turn his car around then with a final wave he turned out of the drive. She didn't close the door immediately she still felt this feeling of foreboding and by keeping the door open it meant that time could stand still.

Veronica closed the door and let out a small gasp. Unbeknown to her Evelyn had come down stairs and was standing by the banister.

"Mother you startled me! Edward has just left for the office I was about to bring you up a cup of tea".

"Sorry my dear, I didn't realise you couldn't hear me walking around upstairs. A cup of tea would be lovely and perhaps a slice of toast and then would it be convenient to sit and talk?"

Veronica breathed out slowly.

"Yes Mother, I think until we talk neither of us are going to get anything out of this week. I will make us a pot of tea and let's get you some toast, butter and marmalade".

Evelyn sat down at the kitchen table and Veronica busied herself getting the tea and toast made. Ten minutes later Evelyn had eaten her breakfast, her daughter quickly cleared the table and stacked the dirty crockery on the draining board waiting for Mrs Davis, the daily help.

"Come on Mother let's make ourselves comfortable, we will go and sit in the lounge".

The central heating was set on a timer and normally by now no one would be at the Chimneys so as the two ladies walked into the lounge Veronica felt a chill in the air. She walked over to the small coffee table placed by one of the two three piece sofas, opening the little drawer she removed a box of matches. After striking the match she knelt in front of the fire place and lit the paper of which the coals and wood had been placed. In a couple of minutes the fire had caught. Veronica beckoned her Mother over to the opposite sofa and with that they both sat down facing each other.

If Veronica had thought that her Mother was going to be reticent then she couldn't be more wrong.

"Veronica this is going to come to you as a great shock, but when I was a practising midwife I did a terrible thing. Terrible doesn't really sum up my deed, but I agreed to a young Mother swapping her baby for another. There hasn't been a day since that I haven't regretted my actions or wondered how it worked out for those innocent people involved".

Veronica opened her mouth to try and say something but nothing came out, but it didn't matter, Evelyn continued.

"It was 1960, April 1960 and I was working at the small private nursing home for Mother's and babies in St Albans. Your Father as you may remember hated me working and only agreed reluctantly because he felt I would be nursing patients who could well afford my services. For some strange reason he thought that the middle classes never had bad luck by having promiscuous daughters. How wrong he was. I didn't as a rule work on a Saturday or Sunday, being a private establishment we midwives organised our own working patterns and it did work well, but this particular weekend I offered to cover for a colleague. On the Thursday and Friday we had six deliveries, two boys and four girls. The rule of the home was that the babies every night would go to the nursery, and in the event of a baby waking to be breast-fed then the baby would be wheeled to the Mother's room. If it was to be bottle fed then we did this in the nursery. There was always an experienced member of staff on this duty because as you can imagine if you weren't swift you could easily have the babies waking each other up with crying. It was about 1.30am and I had to take one of the baby boy's to his Mother. It was her first baby, she was nervous and so I spent 20 minutes with her trying to get her baby to latch on properly. As I left her room I heard another baby crying. This one too needed taking to her Mother, fortunately, a more experienced Mother. All I needed to do was gently wake the Mother and place baby in her arms. Once again on leaving her room another baby had woken. I raced back to find our youngest Mother looking in one of the cots. It wasn't her baby and I wondered what she was doing.

Caroline, you know you shouldn't be in here at night and your baby is in the cot at the end".

"I know, it's this baby she is not breathing!"

"I immediately picked her up. Her little body was cold and she had no colour in her face. I checked her pulse and heartbeat, nothing. I was too late this little mite had died. After placing her back in the cot I made my way to the telephone that was in the nursery for emergencies only. This rang straight through to the night porter whose job it was to make contact with the relevant member of staff. As I went to lift the receiver of the cradle Caroline shouted "Don't, wait! You do know whose baby it is?"

I left the phone and walked over to the cot and then I saw the baby's wrist band,

Baby Cooper.

No this couldn't be happening, not this baby. Her parents had already experienced two still births and several miscarriages. The reason the Mother was delivering in the private hospital wasn't because she chose to be a private patient but she was too frightened to have another delivery in the local General Hospital. My mind was racing. I didn't know what to do I felt as though I was frozen to the spot. Then

Caroline the young Mother spoke with clarity and authority.

"If we swapped the wrist band with my baby's wrist band, they are very similar in colouring and size no one would know. It would be a kindness and it would help".

I started to get annoyed.

"You thoughtless Girl, how can it possibly help?"

"Nurse it would really help and get me out of a scrape and something kind will have come out of all the mess I have caused. Please listen, it will stop my parents from arguing. My baby will be loved by a Mother I have actually met. My parents will pay for the funeral that they believe to be their Granddaughter and I will have her buried so there will always be a mark of her short little life. I am sorry but it is, dare I say perfect. I know that Sylvia has already lost so many babies, she told me. She will be distraught, would you want to be the one to tell her that it has happened again?"

"How would I know that you would never go looking for your baby?"

Caroline now knew that Midwife Compton was beginning to think it could work. "Because my daughter has got to go up for adoption, I reconciled with that at the very beginning of my pregnancy. My parents could never live with a baby born out of wedlock, especially as the Father is one of my parent's oldest friends and

his wife is my Godmother, not that my parents
know that".

The midwife looked at Caroline in disbelief.
"How could you do that to your parents and
come to that, your Godmother?"

Caroline retorted "I didn't think you were
meant to judge".

"I am sorry; please forget I said that, you know
you could never tell anyone, you are 18 now, in
five years, 10, 15 years things might change.
You may want to have contact with her".

"I may have done a really stupid thing but I do
keep my word, no one knows other than you
who the Father is and you don't really know as I
do have two Godmothers who are both
supposedly happily married. My Mother tried
many times to discover who took advantage of
me, that is how my parents saw it, but I made a
really stupid mistake and there is no need to
ruin other people's lives, and perhaps
something good could come out of it".

The whole time Caroline was speaking, Midwife
Compton's heart was racing, could this really
work? Could she believe this totally spoilt girl,
would she keep her promise? The clock was
ticking if they were going to change the name
bands, it was going to have to be now and no
going back.

The room felt cold, Veronica realised she was
staring at her Mother. Evelyn sat still but was

physically and mentally exhausted. The Grandmother clock was ticking loudly in the corner of the room. Was it ticking loudly, or had every other noise just stopped?

Veronica leant across and touched her Mother's hand. She didn't know why but she knew at this moment in time there was nothing she could say. Then like a volcano that was rumbling all of a sudden Veronica opened her mouth and the words just came tumbling out.

"You are telling me you swapped a baby? You gave someone else's baby away? How could you, were you mad".

 Then before she could check her emotions Veronica burst into tears, uncontrollable tears and with that Evelyn got up and gently sat next to her daughter and took her in her arms.

"My Darling daughter I am so sorry for unloading this on to you. It was selfish and wrong of me. I don't suppose you could just forget all about it? No of course not that was a stupid thing to say. Please don't cry anymore. I'll get us a drink, sit still".

The Chimneys rarely saw alcoholic drinks being poured at 11.15 in the morning but this was an exceptional day and Evelyn went to the decanters and poured two glasses of sherry. She handed one of the glasses to her daughter. "Sip it slowly my dear it will warm you up. You must have lots of questions that you need answering but you seem to be in a state of shock and and I think perhaps we should pick this up again tomorrow".

Veronica sipped her sweet sherry not because she wanted to drink it but quite simply because her Mother told her to drink it.

Looking across to her Mother she nodded.

"This is, I think the first time in my life when I am completely lost for words. I don't know whether I should be angry or sad. Quite frankly I don't even know what I can say or do that can even help you. Yes I do need time to digest everything you have said. Let me have time today and we will talk again tomorrow".

If a stranger had been listening to Veronica speaking they would assume that she had been chairing a meeting due to the formality in her voice, not listening to a problem that her Mother had been living with for eighteen years.

Veronica picked up the empty glasses and walked through to her kitchen, placing them on the draining board, she turned as she heard footsteps behind her. It was Mrs Davis,

"Good morning Mrs Cousins. I have stripped and remade the beds and bagged the linen already for collection. If you like I'll tidy the kitchen and sort your supper for tonight. Then a once over for the bathrooms. How does that fit with you? I have to say, funny seeing you here on a Monday morning but nice for me to have a bit of company".

"Yes that all seems perfect. My Mother and I are going to take a turn around the garden then I will start our lunch".

Veronica walked back into the lounge and was unaware of being watched by a startled Mrs Davis. Never before had Mrs Davis heard the word 'perfect' come out of Mrs Cousins mouth, or seen two empty sherry glasses either.

Nothing more was said by Mother or Daughter of what was revealed in the lounge. They both put shoes and coats on and arm in arm they strolled around the garden looking at the spring flowers that had started to look a little sad, soon to be replaced with bedding plants.

The afternoon was spent listening to the afternoon play on radio 4. When Edward came home they all retreated to the kitchen where Veronica continued with the prep that Mrs Davis had started in the morning with that evening's supper.

A number of times in the afternoon and evening before Evelyn retired to her bedroom she glanced at her daughter. If she was truly honest with herself she had been quite shocked at her daughter's distress and was beginning to wonder if she made the right decision in confessing to her. She felt very tired and although many thoughts were buzzing inside her head she immediately fell asleep as soon as her head hit the pillow. It was probably just as well otherwise she would have been sure to have heard her daughter sobbing to her husband in the bedroom at the end of the hallway.

Chapter Eight

Edward on arriving home from the office was unsure as to whether his wife and Mother in Law had had their family business chat. Edward being, as his wife would say a 'typical' man had no illusions that he was capable of noticing any difference in either of the two females. He enjoyed his dinner and the company of his Mother in Law. When Evelyn stated that it was time for her to retire he turned to Veronica. "Darling do you mind if we go up as well it's a long day for me tomorrow, starting with that 9:30am meeting with Bushells".

"Of course not, I'll take Mother up and see you upstairs".

What Edward was not expecting was to find his wife who was sitting on the edge of the bed sobbing her heart out when he walked into their bedroom.

"Darling whatever is the matter? Please don't cry".

Veronica lifted her head and through her tears managed to say." My Mother swapped two babies, she actually swapped two babies. How could she? I feel as though I don't know her. She told me this morning and the rest of the day I felt I was with a total stranger. I think to wait all these years before saying anything means she couldn't have felt any guilt. Perhaps she believed she was dying when she was in Hospital and wanted to clear her conscience before meeting her maker. I just don't know what to think".

Edward had quickly walked to his wife's side and sat and held her. "Tell me what she said from the beginning".

Veronica practically repeated word for word the conversation her Mother had had with her that morning.

Edward realised that he would have to remain unemotional. He suggested that there was still a lot of the story to tell. "If a client had come to see you and wanted your professional help, how would you continue"?

"She isn't a client though she is my Mother, or is she?"

"Veronica that is a really silly thing to say, of course she is your Mother. She really does need your help and you should feel flattered that she has confided in you. I know it is huge what she has told you but you need to stop looking at her as your Mother, and instead as a client. You need to step back. There is a lot more to tell. Are you sure talking here is the best place for you? I don't mean taking her into your chambers but would it be better if when you talk next it's somewhere, for want of a better word 'new'?"

Edward could see that Veronica was now composed and was thinking of somewhere they could go.

"I am sorry Darling but I have really got a difficult day ahead". He quickly added" and so have you so let's get some sleep and start the new day fresh and bushy tailed".

Fifteen minutes later they were both in bed. The bedside lights had been turned off and Veronica snuggled into her husband's arms. It wasn't long before she could hear the gentle snoring that he made. While listening to this familiar sound she too fell into a deep sleep.

Chapter Nine

The next day wasn't the kind of day you would want to go on a little jaunt. Veronica and Edward awoke to heavy rain beating against their bedroom window. Edward turned to look at the time 6am. He turned off the alarm clock that was set for 6.15am. No point keeping that on. He got out of bed turned and kissed Veronica on the forehead.

"I am going to get up now, any chance of you making breakfast so I can eat soon as I have shaved and showered?"

"No problem Darling, I'll go down now, bacon and eggs or would prefer just toast".

"Bacon and eggs and anything else you can squeeze on the plate, not sure if am going to get any lunch today".

Edward by now was in the en-suite, another idea they had seen at the Ideal home exhibition. Mrs Davis had said when the master bedroom and en- suite had been finished by the decorators, that it should be photographed for a glossy magazine.

Veronica called after him. "I do wish you would make sure of a lunch break. Now you are approaching fifty I am not sure that a traditional

English breakfast is the right way to start the day".

She could hear Edward laughing as she put her dressing gown and slippers on and made her way downstairs to the kitchen. It was when she saw her Mother's handbag by the kitchen table that yesterday came flooding back to her. What was she to do? Edward had suggested going out but where on this miserable wet day? Then she knew, a twenty minute drive away was a coast road. As you turn around one of the bends there is a parking bay which over looks the sea. Its main use is for holiday makers to take in the view at the first sighting of the sea on their way down to the Sussex coast. It was really meant for a five minute stop but at this time of the year no one else would be around, so they could comfortably sit and talk and, yes, she would take a flask of coffee as well.

By time Edward had come downstairs his breakfast was ready and his wife was looking much happier than the night before. He also noticed the flask on the breakfast bar.

"Off to somewhere nice?"

"Well yes actually, I have taken you up on your idea of speaking to Mother somewhere neutral that I know she has never been to, Beachcombers viewing point. What do you think, she won't see much. It will be much too misty but it is somewhere peaceful where we can talk".

Edward eating his breakfast felt a new calmness and control had now come over Veronica.

"Darling, that is an excellent idea! I am sure you can sort this out. I'll finish my breakfast and then I am off". Looking at the kitchen clock he leapt up from the table and taking his suit jacket from behind his chair he leant forward to kiss Veronica on the cheek.

"Is that the time, I really must be off, love you. I will ring and let you know what time I expect to be home".

With that he was gone out of the door.

Veronica looked around and decided that today was probably going to be harder than yesterday so what was the best way to start it. 'Breakfast in bed for Mother and I will join her'. With a laden tray of coffee, grapefruit, toast, marmalade and butter, Veronica made her way upstairs.

By 10 o'clock Veronica had made the flask and added a packet of chocolate biscuits to the bag, moved her car from the garage and parked as near to the front door as possible as it was still raining.

Chapter Ten

Five minutes later Veronica and Evelyn were driving through the countryside. Both were silent. Veronica thinking that it would be best to let her Mother take the lead. Evelyn was relieved she wanted to keep the story straight in her head and to do this she felt concentration was needed. After five minutes of driving the rain was easing off and by time Veronica pulled into Beachcombers viewing point the rain had stopped. The window wipers went across the windscreen and cleared the moisture off but the view was one of thick mist. Veronica wound her window down slightly and the sound of the sea below could be heard. The cove wasn't rocky so there was no smashing of waves breaking but instead a much gentler relaxing sound.

Veronica turned to her Mother,

"I bought a flask of coffee would you like a cup now".

"No dear, I think it best if we talk or, I talk. I need to tell you everything because it changed our lives, all of ours. As I said I shouldn't have been on duty that evening I had swapped with a colleague and because of that it had caused a rift with your Father. That week we had been invited to have dinner with all of his partners and wives. As you know he hated not being able to be agreeable to invitations and when it wasn't possible for me to either change back or find someone else he was annoyed, so when I left for the Hospital it was with a heavy heart and as you can imagine I was in no mood for a difficult duty. When I arrived, Dora, you do remember Auntie Dora?"

Evelyn never waited for a reply but carried on. "Well she did the handover".

Then much to Veronica's horror her Mother started to cry. She reached into the bag the flask was in and produced a box of paper hankies. Taking one from the box she gently wiped her Mother's face. Then waited for her to speak.

Very quietly Evelyn continued.

"Dora was very bubbly when I walked into our little office, in fact she could hardly contain herself to tell me".

"The baby that is going to be adopted! Well by looking at the Grandparents today during visiting, I think that baby may be going home with its Mother".

"I remember asking her how could that work, her parents had titles. Not easy to introduce an illegitimate baby into the family. Had it been anyone else other than Dora I wouldn't have paid any attention, but as you remember she wasn't one for fancy ideas. Strange as it may seem it wasn't unheard of for a baby being put up for adoption in the private nursing home. We had both seen a number of young girls' parents who had obviously used their savings to allow the baby to be born in an upmarket environment. Perhaps hoping the baby would be placed into a better home, I don't know. You see I knew that when I agreed to go along with Caroline's plan, there was a chance she could have actually kept her baby. If she had been able to keep her baby her life was sure to be more complete than it has been. I couldn't tell her because if Dora had got the situation wrong and her baby did go up for adoption then it would be to a couple she would never meet. At least this way she had sort of chosen the parents herself. I reluctantly agreed to go along with Caroline's idea, my head was in a whirl until I realised the babies had to have new wrist bands. That was easy the name bands then were not very secure and we always kept a supply in the nursery so I wrote out two new ones and took the old ones off. Before you ask I felt sick holding baby Cooper's little wrist and cutting through her wrist band but time was of the essence. If anyone had walked past they could have seen us, the nursery walls were glass. Caroline played her part well as the grieving Mother, but then she was grieving, she had just given her baby away".

Veronica wound her window up, she felt chilly. Reaching for the bag again she took out the flask and lowered the compartment door on the dash board. It had two moulded holes suitable for flask cups. After filling the cups and putting the flask back in the bag, she produced the chocolate digestive biscuits. She passed one of the biscuits to her Mother.

"Mum, do you remember when I was a teenager and was panicking over exams, you would make me a hot drink and with it, give me a chocolate digestive and say this will settle your worries. Well I am probably not as naïve as that now but you do need some sustenance come on eat up".

Mother and Daughter ate their biscuits and drank their cups of steaming hot coffee, both not sure what to say next.

How much longer they sat like this neither of them would have been able to say but eventually Veronica spoke.

"Mother, if I could grant you a wish to make all this right for you, what would you, wish for? "

"My dear there is two things I really would like to do, but both I think impossible.

I would like to see where the baby was buried and see for myself that Caroline kept her promise about the grave, and for me to pay my respects to that tiny little mite. Secondly I would like to see how Caroline is. Did she turn her life around? She was a very bright and quite a beautiful girl but she wouldn't have been the first to have thrown all of that away. I need to know whether she was able to move on". Veronica looked at her Mother with a quizzical look

 "But what about the baby who you gave away you haven't mentioned her. Don't you want to know what became of her? How her life is turning out?"

"No dear, she wasn't a victim. You see that couple really wanted to have a little baby. If they hadn't they would never have gone through so many pregnancies. She was going to be loved and cared for and really that is all any of us can ask for".

Veronica thought it time to change tack.

"Mum, you said that it changed all of our lives how was that? Michael had just qualified as a Doctor and I had left home. I was married and had started my career as a Solicitor. It's not like you and Father separated over it. Did you tell Father?"

Evelyn looked shocked. "No, of course not. He would never have been able to understand. That was something I was very sure about. What I had done had to stay with me. A number of times before we moved I would wake up during the night and I always said the same words.' What have I done, oh no what have I done?' Your Father would tell me what I had said but never asked why. Veronica, if I hadn't rambled on in the hospital we wouldn't be having this conversation now. I told Caroline that she must never speak of it and I had to make the same promise. It's just in the hospital I was calling out those same words. What if it was to happen again, next time I could say something far more damaging and break my word to Caroline, and who knows what trouble that would cause? Remember Caroline is still in her 30's. What was it you asked me? Oh yes I remember, it was because of that night that I gave up midwifery and eventually your Father and I bought the Willows.

Even now I can't remember much after changing the wrist bands and calling the night porter to inform the Obstetrician on call. The procedure was to take the baby out of the nursery, so I pushed her in her little cot into the sluice. It was always a very warm room due to the hot water tank in there. Other babies then started to wake for their feeds and it seemed within minutes the Consultant was there. He pronounced her dead and did the necessary paperwork. I had to make a report for the coroner just in case some where along the line some one thought there had been any form of foul play and that is all I can remember. I think someone else must have taken on my duties as I really can't remember looking after the babies for the rest of my shift.

Living With The Consequences

My next duty wasn't until the following Thursday and by then Caroline and Mrs Cooper had both been discharged. I can't say I wasn't relieved that they had both gone home but even so it was so hard to go into the nursery and not relive that moment when the babies were swapped. Having always loved all aspects of midwifery my dream job was over.

Years before I had always thought how lovely it would be to run your own residential care home. When it was clear to your Father my life needed a new challenge he readily agreed that we should do something together. It turned out that the reason why all the partners had been invited to that dinner party was because Gerald, the senior partner, wanted too retire almost immediately. At the time nobody knew why but sadly he died six months later of cancer. That seemed to cause an avalanche. Roger and his wife, can't remember her name, also wanted to leave. He had always fancied himself as a bit of a countryman and saw this as an opportunity to make a dream come true and buy a farm. That left three accountants out of five. Well the other two were always a little too thick with each other and your Father was always uncertain of their integrity and honesty so that was a good enough reason for him to sell his share. Once that was done we started to look for somewhere suitable. It didn't take long as I had already started to look. Within four weeks of that awful time I had worked my notice, and had nothing else to do. Of course everyone thought I just couldn't get over the shock of finding baby Cooper. Silly really, after all death is sadly all part of nursing whatever your job but, well it was for the best they thought that was the reason".

Veronica shifted in her seat. This revelation from her Mother was mentally exhausting and she felt that that both of them had enough for the day.

"Look Mum, why don't I turn the car around and we'll head for home. I am becoming a bit stiff and starting to feel I need a comfort stop. We can pick up again later on during the week and in the mean time I can have a think to see if there is anything I can do to help".

Evelyn touched her daughter's hand." You are helping already by listening to me. It's true what they say, a trouble shared is a troubled halved".

Veronica turned the ignition on, expertly did a three point turn, and headed for home.

That night Evelyn went to bed at 9pm. She thanked Veronica for her support and wished her and Edward a good night's sleep. Only when Veronica could hear her Mother walking around the bedroom upstairs did she turn to Edward.

"Darling you know it isn't my place to tell you what Mother and I have been discussing today but you were right, there was more to tell. I really want to do something to help".

"Well at the moment she thinks you are helping, she thanked you for your support".

"Yes I know, but I don't feel it is enough, unless".

Edward repeated her last word "Unless?"

Veronica's face lit up. "I have got it, I know what I can do! Do you remember Harold Brownlow? He was a retired Chief Inspector from the Metropolitan police and occasionally we, the firm, would use him to do delicate snooping for lack of a better word. Well I wonder if he would do a little snooping for Mum?"

Edward looked surprised "Didn't you replace Harold when he retired from your employment".

"Yes we did, and Stan is fine but this is Mum's business and I feel that complete discretion is vital".

"Do you know Darling in all the years I have known you, you have never called your Mother 'Mum'?"

Veronica smiled, "yes it is strange isn't it, if nothing else happens with all of this business, it will have made Mum and I much closer".

After a very dismal, wet and windy Tuesday, Wednesday proved to be the complete opposite. The sun was shining and the birds singing as everyone at the Chimneys awoke.

Edward wasn't in such a rush for the office this morning and was enjoying a leisurely breakfast with Veronica and Evelyn.

"So ladies, what have you planned for today?"

Veronica was chewing a slice of toast so Evelyn answered,

"I am happy to do nothing or anything Veronica would like to do. She is on annual leave and I really don't expect her to devote all her time to me".

Veronica, having finished chewing was pleased to be able to tell her Mother that she had a little plan of her own, which, in time if proved to be fruitful, may help both of her Mother's dilemmas.

"Mum I do have a little job to do, it shouldn't take long but while I am doing that would you like to go to my hairdressers and have your hair done? Then this afternoon we could go to the gardens at Everleigh and have afternoon tea, what do you think?"

"Yes an excellent idea and perhaps a little trim as well. I do like Carol, you know, the hairdresser who comes into the home but, sometimes I do think her cutting makes me look a little old ladyish".

Veronica and Edward laughed after all Evelyn was exactly that, an old lady, but only in age and not in spirit.

Chapter Eleven

The following day Harold Brownlow was sitting having a cup of coffee with his wife. They lived in a very neat and tidy bungalow ten miles from Blakedon. His neighbours all admired his manicured lawn and often commented that his flowers and plants looked as though they were standing to attention. It was of no surprise to any of them that this smartly dressed man had served both in the army and the Metropolitan police force.

The letterbox rattled and there was a tiny thud on the door mat. Harold started to rise from his chair.

"Sounds like the postman has been".

Before his wife could answer he was already making his way to the door.

She called after him.

"Anything for me? I am still waiting for that knitting pattern I ordered".

"Sorry dear, there is a gas bill, it looks like a reminder for my car to be serviced and and what's this, a letter to me".

Harold came back into the lounge with the post and sat down. He placed the gas bill and car service reminder on the coffee table and started to gently open the other envelope. He had scrutinised the hand writing as he was walking back down the hall but had no idea who it was from. After slipping the letter out of the envelope he immediately went to the bottom of the sheet of paper to see who had signed it.

"Well I never! it's from Veronica Cousins, one of the partners from the solicitors Wallace, Featherby and Cousins. Now why is she writing to me?"

Edna, Harold's wife knew that this was a rhetorical question of which he was expecting no answer. When you have been married for over forty years there are some things you instinctively know.

Five minutes passed and Harold had still made no comment and by now Edna was becoming a little curious.

Thinking Harold now needed a little nudge, she asked.

"Not bad news, I hope".

It worked Harold looked up." No not bad news, it's, well, confidential. Mrs Cousins makes that quite clear, but she wonders if I would undertake a little job for her she hasn't said what it is. She only says it's private work but understands if I don't want to have a small break from my retirement. She will pay all my expenses, time and if satisfactory a small bonus. Now what do you make of that?"

Before Edna could answer Harold was making his way back into the hall, and the next thing Edna heard was the lifting of the telephone receiver. She always had a foreboding of listening to private conversations so she got up and gently pushed the door closed. She didn't have to wait long until Harold was back in the lounge.

"Well, I hope you don't mind dear but tomorrow I have arranged to go and see Mrs Cousins in Blakedon. I didn't think we had anything arranged?"

"Perfectly fine, do you think you will be back for lunch?"

"Oh yes definitely, it's more of a briefing, probably will take me longer to get there and back".

Chapter Twelve

Veronica's little plan was quite simply to contact Harold Brownlow. After some thought she felt it better to write to him. This way she could control exactly what she wanted to say. As a Solicitor she was well versed in this but dealing with her Mother's problem somehow made it very different.

The letter was not going to contain any details of the job it was basically asking him if he was interested and if so, asking him to call on her home phone number, anytime that week or business hours thereafter.

Veronica was delighted to answer the phone and hear Harold Brownlow's clear voice on the other end. She asked him how Edna and he were keeping and told him that the business was completely private. This had never been a problem for Harold as Edna had always been respectful of his work. With that agreed Veronica asked Harold to the Chimneys for a meeting and both happily agreed that it should be the following day at 11am.

The following morning at 10 minutes to eleven Veronica and Evelyn settled in the lounge side by side on one of the settees. In front of them a coffee table had been positioned, waiting for the laden tray in the kitchen. Friday was one of Mrs Davis's days and she had already been instructed that when she heard Mrs Compton's guest arrive she was to make coffee and bring it in to the lounge. Then, take herself upstairs and give both the boys bedrooms a thorough clean already for the Easter holidays when they would be home from boarding school. Mrs Davis knew that this job had been given to her so she couldn't possibly hear any of the conversation in the lounge, which puzzled her because how could there be any wrong doings going on when Mrs Cousins own Mother was going to be present?

At 5 minutes to eleven a car could be heard coming up the drive, it stopped, someone got out, closed the car door. The door bell rang, Veronica looked at her Mother.

"You are sure you want to go ahead with this, it isn't too late to change your mind".

"Veronica, thank you for asking but I think you should let that poor man in, he will begin to wonder if anyone is at home".

Veronica touched her Mother's hand as she passed and went to the front door.

"Good morning Mr Brownlow, so kind of you to come, and at such short notice"

"It's good to see you again Mrs Cousin's".

Then the lounge door closed and Mrs Davis heard no more. As instructed she made the coffee and put the pot on the tray. She didn't need to call out that the door needed opening with parquet flooring her footsteps could be heard. Veronica opened the door and allowed Mrs Davis to place the tray on the coffee table. Veronica thanked her and Mrs Davis retreated closing the door behind her. She picked up her box of polishes and cloths from the kitchen and made her way upstairs wondering to herself as to whether she should have curtsied on her way out, and then gave a little chuckle to herself.

Veronica, on entering the lounge with Harold, introduced him to her Mother. Evelyn immediately felt herself relaxing. Harold was indeed a very tall, slim good looking man but carried an air of authority. He also had kind blue eyes and a hint of a smile, someone Evelyn could relate to.

Veronica started to pour the coffee and while she did this Evelyn felt that she needed to control the meeting. She was aware that they were in her daughter's home but this was her mess and she didn't want her daughter to feel responsible.

"Mr Brownlow, for reasons that I don't really want to discuss at the moment I would like you to try and find a young lady who very briefly played a part in my life. She was very young only eighteen, and so now would be in her mid thirties. She was also unmarried so that could have easily have changed. There are two parts to the job. The second part sounds macabre, but I would like a grave located. Is that at all possible?"

Harold leant forward and took the coffee cup offered to him by Veronica.

"Mrs Compton, can I ask, is the grave anything to do with the young lady? Because if it is then I think it would be better for me to accept the undertaking to find her first. The reason I suggest this is that it is always possible that she herself may tell you what you want to know. I am sure that it would be better all round if that were to happen".

Evelyn who was intently listening immediately answered.

"If you think that is best then we will be guided by you, as you are the professional".

"That's very kind of you to say. Now all I need is the name of the young lady and perhaps a possible address from when you knew her".

Evelyn started to feel a bit uncomfortable as she had no idea of Caroline's address.

Veronica seeing her Mother's discomfort stepped in.

"My Mother can give you the County is that enough information for you?"

"That isn't a problem, it will give me a starting point".

Getting out a small black note book with a very slim pencil pushed into the spine, Harold asked Evelyn the name he would be researching. Evelyn looked a little hesitant and then with a large breath repeated her previous statement. "Well she was only 18 and unmarried so of course her name could have changed by now but she was Caroline Elizabeth Sowersby Smyth and she was living in Hertfordshire".

Harold, busily writing, looked up. "That is an unusual surname do you happen to know by chance her Father's occupation"?

"Yes I do, he was a High Court Judge, does that matter?"

"No it doesn't matter, in fact it should make my task a lot easier. You see I can probably find her through her Father. I should correct myself, I don't mean approach her Father. It follows that if some one is connected to a prominent person then this can give us a lead. Right, is that all clear any questions so far?"

Evelyn looked at her daughter and they both nodded in agreement that they were satisfied so far.

Harold continued." The next step is for me to ask whether or not when supposing I find our young lady, you want me to make some kind of contact. Now let's just step back to me finding her. There is a possibility she may be living abroad short term, has emigrated or sadly passed away abroad. If any of these possibilities has happened then my task may even become impossible. Now looking to a more positive outcome, if I find her how you would like me to proceed? There are a couple of options; I can conveniently bump into her and try find out the lay of the land or I could speak to her on your behalf. That is all supposing that at some stage you would like to meet her yourself. Now I understand that is a lot to think about so there is no pressure to tell me now".

If Harold was surprised with the speed in which Evelyn answered he showed no signs.

"I would very much like to meet her again but it has got to be with her complete agreement and certainly no shocks or surprises".

"I totally understand Mrs Compton. Now how would you like me to keep in touch? I can write to either or both of you. The difficulty with that is the delay and I find that when somebody makes a decision to get involved in this kind of research that they want answers as soon as possible. If that doesn't work for you then the other option is the telephone. Now would that be to both of you or just one and which one?" This was one thing Mother and Daughter hadn't discussed and Harold looking at them could see neither of them wanted to make the decision.

"Ok, as it is really your business Mrs Compton how would it be if I relayed my findings to you? Then you can discuss it with Mrs Cousins and either of you then can get back to me".

Veronica looked pleased. Yes, it was right that Harold should deal with her Mother, and then a thought crossed her mind.

"Mother, how would you take the call at the Willows. I know the communal phone in the hallway is in a booth but it isn't very private. I suppose you could take the calls in the Manager's office but to do that you would have to say it's private and the last thing you want to do is unsettle the staff".

"Veronica you are quite right. Taking a call from Mr Brownlow in the home just won't work, far better for you to receive the calls and then we can discuss it and I am happy for you to get back to him".

"That is fine ladies, sounds like a sensible plan. Now thank you for thinking of me and trusting me to be able to help. That was a lovely cup of coffee but if you don't mind I will be on my way as I am already working out the best way to proceed".

After a few more pleasantries, Harold left, he was already forming a plan but first, home and lunch. Then he was going to retire to his study and make a start.

Chapter Thirteen

Harold, with a cup of coffee went into his study. It was just after two o'clock and he needed to make a phone call, but first he wanted to locate the direct phone number. What Harold never let on to Evelyn and Veronica was that Sowersby-Smyth was a name he was familiar with. Asking the profession of the girl's father was just confirmation, not too many Sowersby-Smyth's around.

Harold had served in the Metropolitan police and as such worked on some high profile cases which as a consequence were tried at the Old Bailey and, on a number of occasions in front of High Court Judge Sowersby-Smyth.

Whether it was his time in the army or that he was just tidy and organised, but the address book he needed was at the bottom of the drawer exactly where he was expecting to find it.

He rang the number and waited, from experience he knew this might take a little time. A young girl answered.

"Hello, Switchboard The Times".

"Hello, Back numbers please".

In seconds a voice answered. "Back numbers".

"Good afternoon John, Harold Brownlow here, how are you?"

"Very well Sir, and you and your good lady?"

"We are both keeping well, no complaints. I was wondering if you could possibly help me. I suppose I should have been put through to reference library but you have always been able to put your hands on what I am looking for, so have you anything recent on Judge Sowersby-Smyth, any little bit of tittle tattle, you know the kind of thing?"

John Pritchard, the back numbers man for the Times, smiled to himself. It had been awhile since Chief inspector Brownlow had retired and had been after some information. On a number of occasions John Pritchard had been of use to Harold and the Metropolitan police. He had an avid interest in criminal activity and justice which he read in depth from the newspapers he archived.

"It sounds as though you didn't know he passed away, oh about year ago I would say. Now let me think, February 1977, yes that's about right. Had a heart attack and died almost instantly, he had only been fully retired a matter of months, strange you didn't know anything about it? It was quite a big thing at the time. The papers listed a number of big cases he sat in on, I know he was retired but I bet a few criminals were relieved he had gone, he wasn't a lenient man, not that that is a bad thing".

Harold laughed "Quite right, if you are saying February last year then my wife and I were out of the country. We decided to do that trip of a life time and spent four months out in Australia. Spent some time with the wife's brother, he emigrated about 15 years ago and then did a bit of sightseeing. So Sowersby-Smyth passed away then, was there an obituary?"

"Yes, if I remember rightly a nice little piece about him and his family but I will dig it all out and send it to you".

"Excellent John, thank you very much".

"Thank you Sir and don't worry it's on the house, you have brightened my day up, take care".

With that Harold put the phone down now all he had to do was wait for the old copies of the Times to arrive and then plan his next step.

Chapter Fourteen

I am not sure if I am more excited than my Daughter but I couldn't be more proud. She has worked so hard over the years and this September she will be setting off for her first year at University. English literature is her chosen subject which, had I been given a choice, is the path I would have chosen. It's funny because although I was born into a privileged family and money was never an issue my life was very restricted.

I am now coming into my late 30's surrounded by a supportive family, but it wasn't always like that. My arrival into the world was thought by Mother to be no less than a miracle. At 39 years of age she had given up all hope of another baby. My Mother married my Father when she was 19 and had a big society wedding. My Father was becoming a noted man of the law and fourteen years older than my Mother. I wonder now if she had been looking for more of a Father figure than a husband but it's not something you can ask. My Mother, right up to my Father's death, never really stood up to him. For me this was unfortunate because I did try but it is hard to do so when you are continually told that being a girl, education wasn't really needed. Not any higher level anyway. I am digressing. When my Mother was 20 my brother Richard Charles Sowersby-Smyth was born. Apparently my Father doted on him. Although spoilt by my Father he turned out to be the perfect son and I should say, older brother.

By time I was old enough to realise I had a brother he was already planning to go to university reading law just as Father had done or the Royal Airforce if the Second World War was still raging on. Luckily for us Richard was never called up for active service and did his time in National Service, but it still meant that we barely saw each other while I was a little girl.

My home was a big Victorian house on the edge of a village. We had a lovely village school which I attended until I was 10 years old. Then my Mother needed to go into hospital for a Hysterectomy. This was one of the many occasions when what my Father said, went. His view was that it wouldn't be possible for me to remain at home. My Mother would need three months convalescence. We had a housekeeper come- cook who lived in. My Mother also employed two ladies part-time from the village who tended to all the other domestic duties within the house. With that amount of staff I felt sure I could stay at home. It was a very sad time for me with Mother going into hospital. I was sent away to a new school for the summer term. It was unusual for a child to start a new school during a term back then, normally the time for new starters was in September. My biggest hardship was that all the children in the village were my friends. Saying this, they were never invited to my home but it was acceptable for some to play in our garden, weather permitting. Of course my behaviour when I was told this fait accompli was not good but that didn't matter, in fact my Father used it to quantify why it was best that I was sent away. My school in Surrey turned out to be a dream. My fear of sharing a bedroom was never a problem the dormitories had curtained cubicles and there was only eight of us to each dorm. Our Headmistress was very pro education for all females and also had the belief that if we worked hard then we should play hard. So all sports were encouraged. Even girls who weren't particularly sporty managed to find something they liked. Yes dear old Miss Richardson was an all rounder.

From the age of 10 to 18 I was extremely happy. I enjoyed learning, sports and made many friends. My school reports were always excellent and I was happy, learning as much as I could with the belief that I would one day have a career of my own, just like my Father, and my brother who was now becoming a very successful Solicitor.

It was just before my eighteenth birthday when I was home from school for the Easter holidays that I realised all of my education would be wasted. I had spent time each day revising for my national exams on my return to school, when casually at dinner my Father asked how I had spent my day. When I had explained that it was spent studying he just raised his eyebrows. It was months later that I found out what that had meant.

My last term at school was hard. It was a particularly hot summer and we were cooped up in the school hall with all the windows open hearing the younger girls having fun on the playing fields, while we were taking our exams . I had so much riding on this. I really wanted to do well.

During the last week of term all the upper six girls had an interview with Miss Richardson. Mine went well. She had no doubt that my results would be good and that higher education, if I was interested, was a must. I told her that studying English literature was my aim but what I would do with it after I still didn't know. Her advice was, 'one step at a time'.

My last day of term was sad but also exciting. In September I would be off to pastures new, and University.

Chapter Fifteen

Then it happened, on my second day home.
Father was home to lunch which was quite
unusual. My Mother was asking if I would like
the use of her car when, Father looked at me,
and quite bluntly told me that he didn't agree
with women having careers. Mother and he had
agreed that I would do the season as a
debutante and then very likely be engaged to
be married, married! What was he saying 'be
married' I was only 18! To his annoyance my
napkin went on the table and I left the room.
It was a beautiful day and I needed to get my
head straight. How was I going to tackle my
parents after the revelation at lunch time. I
chose to go across the fields to the side of our
rear garden. Things were not getting any clearer
in my head. I seemed to be going around in
circles. After the second field is a road. While
waiting to cross it, a car drove past. All of a
sudden I could hear the screech of brakes and
when I looked up Uncle Derek was waving to
me. He wasn't a blood relative, he was a friend
of my father's and married to one of my
Godmothers.
He called out and asked if I wanted a lift.

I wasn't in any hurry to get home so after discovering that he was actually test driving the car, I asked if it would be alright to tag a long. The afternoon turned out to be quite good fun. After he returned the car to the dealer we went for tea. Uncle Derek or, 'Derek' as he said I should now call him, was very sympathetic to my cause but made it quite clear that he couldn't take sides. I reassured him that it was nice to be able to speak to someone who could remain neutral.

Looking at his watch he said that he was supposed to be at the railway station five minutes ago collecting my Godmother. I assured him that it was a twenty minute walk home which I was capable of doing on my own and thanked him for tea. With that he was off. For the next couple of weeks, when ever I went for a walk, which I frequently did as the atmosphere with my parents was awful, I would bump into Derek. For an eighteen year old he was good to be with. He would listen to me without judging, he calmed me when I was angry and he comforted me when I was upset. The last time he saw me walking along and offered me a ride, the comforting went too far. I was consenting but part of me knew it was wrong and wanted him to stop. For all my bravado I was naïve and had absolutely no idea how I could get him to stop. Since that last ride in his car I have grown to realise that I wouldn't have been the first young girl he had taken advantage of. He was Father's accountant, how did he manage to spend his afternoons driving around the countryside! My Godmother Auntie Marjory adored him. It was only after Derek died of a heart attack 18 months after I gave my baby away that I discovered my Father tolerated him because strangely enough he was a good accountant. My Mother apparently always felt guilty because it was her who introduced Auntie Majorie to him. It was certainly love for Auntie Marjory. For him it was money. She was financially very well of and not the prettiest girl at the party, nor the slimmest but by far the wealthiest. Ironically they never had any children so she treated him like a spoilt child.

I had felt let down now, cheap and very weepy. Fortunately for me the weather had deteriorated so I didn't have to make up any excuses for not going out. Then six weeks after that fateful drive, my exam results arrived. Our postman was early that morning and the envelope was waiting for me in the dinning room next to my cup and saucer. I could barely look at my parents as I felt so guilty about my behaviour with Derek. I had no enthusiasm in opening the envelope, but they were both watching me. I slipped the thin piece of paper out and to my surprise I had passed everything with top grades. It was all too much, I bent my head over and sobbed uncontrollably.

Eventually my Mother got up from the table and helped me up. Still sobbing, she took me upstairs to my room. Then I heard her from the hall, she was ringing our Doctor. She came back upstairs with tea and toast on a tray and then sat next to me on the bed.

"Never mind dear, I am sure you did your best. The academic life isn't for everyone".

I looked up in total surprise, she had actually thought I had failed!

"Mother, I have passed everything with flying colours ".

Then I burst into tears again, I just had no control. Poor Mother, she looked completely at a loss.

It wasn't long after that the door bell rang and I heard Mrs Bennett open the front door. I could hear her invite our Doctor in.

I turned to look at my Mother.

"Don't worry darling, Dr Fellows will know what's best. I will bring him up to you".

"Mother I don't want to see the Doctor I am not Ill. Why did you ring him?"

It was no use. Within a minute I could hear her greeting our G.P.

Chapter Sixteen

He was with me it seemed, for ages. All I could think was that he had left his surgery with ailing patients to come and see me. I had never really thought much about what a GP really did other than see the sick but he was just so kind. I hadn't intended to tell him anything but ended up telling him everything. After a brief examination which he asked if I would like my Mother present and I vehemently said no, he gently told me that he suspected I was pregnant. He couldn't be a hundred percent sure because it was too early but everything about me suggested I was.

"But it was only once?" I remember shouting at him.

"I am afraid Caroline, that is all it takes. Would you like me to tell your parents?"

"Oh God no, they don't have to know do they?"

"I think we both know that it would be best to tell them, and then plans can be made".

Even then looking back I think I had realised that I was pregnant and had already decided that a termination was out of the question. That's how it was. He left me and spoke with my parents. I chose not to come out of my room for two weeks. All my meals were sent up. I only came out to use the bathroom next door. By time my pregnancy was confirmed, my parents had already had two weeks to decide my fate. The plan of me becoming a debutante was now forgotten. After Dr Fellows had confirmed my pregnancy in the morning I was summoned to my Father's study. I knocked at the door and my Father called me in. It was a fairly brief interview with my Father sitting in front of his large desk, my Mother standing behind him and a chair was positioned to the side of his desk. I sat down, barely looking up. During the whole miserable five minutes not once was my condition mentioned. It was made clear that the arrangements were not up for negotiation. The following day Mother was to drive me to my Aunt Constance's, one of Father's three sisters. She was a widow and lived in Norfolk in a small village five miles from Kings Lynn. There I was to stay until it was time for me to go into hospital. At this time I would be a private patient at the nearest maternity hospital. When I had fully recovered from this stay, then, and only then could I come home. Mother and I duly left the next morning for Norfolk. The rest of the previous day was spent packing; clothes, books, my record player and records.

Chapter Seventeen

Aunt Constance had always been my most favourite of Aunts. When I was four years old and she had been recently widowed, Mother and I went to stay with her for the summer. She was two years older than Father but always seemed much younger, in fact more my Mother's age. Even though she was grieving for Uncle Arthur she made our stay fun.

Mother stayed overnight and after a hearty breakfast (because whether you liked it or not Aunt Constance always fed her guests well) my Mother left for home.
It didn't take long for us to fall into a routine. Rather like at home there was a housekeeper and daily cleaners who were always very polite and never looked down at me (it didn't take them long to realise why I was there).
Once a week I either had a visit from the local GP or the community midwife. I had no interest in going out. Aunt Constance's house was set in four acres of garden. Any exercise I needed, I'd take a stroll around the garden. When Aunt Constance entertained, I stayed upstairs. She very kindly had one of the many bedrooms

turned into a lounge/dining room so I could be quite self contained. Looking back It's funny during the time I spent in Norfolk not one of my friends made contact with me and I didn't really think about them, I was too ashamed. I suppose Mother and Father had taken care of that problem as well.

By time I was 36 weeks my anxiety over the delivery had began to show. I couldn't eat or sleep properly and when anyone was to ask what was the matter I would just burst into floods of tears. My weight was now dropping and Aunt Constance was worried over my health. After another two weeks my Aunt phoned my Father and was insistent that I should return home, so that is what happened. Mother came up to drive me back to my home. Before she arrived I made my Aunt promise that she would ring me often so as to make sure I wasn't being abandoned to some awful unmarried Mother's home. She readily agreed as she knew that would never happen. In my state of mind I could still hear my Father's words that I was not to return until everything was over.

I said a tearful goodbye to Aunt Constance feeling extremely guilty after everything she had done for me and she made me promise that fairly soon I would return to her for a holiday.

On the drive home, Mother explained the plan. My parents had told the story that as I was considering becoming a nurse and I'd decided at very short notice to help nurse my elderly Aunt. Somehow while administering to her every need I had been struck down with glandular fever so was returning home. However because of the illness, I needed isolation and bedrest so would only be looked after by my Mother. Then when the Doctor thought it was the appropriate time I would be admitted to the private maternity home in St.Albans to await the delivery of the baby. The baby would then be given up for adoption via the maternity home. The new plan worked well. After twelve days back in my own surroundings our family GP thought it advisable for my stay to start at St.Agnes's. The following day when our housekeeper Mrs Bennett had a dental appointment, Mother and I with my case which had been packed ready for over a week, left for the maternity hospital. At this stage it felt like a bad dream that was soon going to be over. On our arrival we were shown my room, which would be mine for the whole of my stay. It was rather pleasant and had a view of a very small garden to the rear.

Within forty eight hours I had gone into labour. Not really knowing what to expect I had woken with tummy pains at three o'clock thinking it

was the orange I had eaten during the evening.
On examination the midwife immediately called
the porter for me to be taken to the delivery
suite.

I have been told many times since then that a
seven hour labour for a first baby was good but
it hurt like hell. The pain in my back was
excruciating and it would have been so nice to
have had perhaps my Mother holding my hand
and reassuring me but back in 1960 you had no
such luxuries. At 10 past 10 my baby was
delivered. A healthy 7lb 4oz baby girl, born on
Friday 8th April.

Did I bond with her straight away? I really don't
know? Most of the time I slept. Never having
felt so tired before and with all the loss of sleep
I had suffered the last weeks of my stay with
Aunt Constance. I remember that when I was
awake all I wanted to do was to keep going to
have a look at her in the nursery so I could fix in
my mind exactly what she looked like. After all I
was told that after four days she would be
taken away.

Much to my surprise, both my parents visited
on the Saturday afternoon, and more
surprisingly my Mother insisted on seeing her
Granddaughter. After sitting with me for an
hour they both were taken to the nursery. How
long they stayed with their Grand daughter I
don't remember but, by time they had returned
I had fallen asleep again. My Mother gently

woke me, she appeared to be quite tearful and even my Father looked regretful. Their farewells were extremely warm and both promised to visit the following day.

I don't consider myself to be forceful but when something happens that in my view is extremely important then I manage to get this extra strength from somewhere, which unbeknown to me was going to happen that very evening. The nursing staff were becoming a little concerned with the amount of time I spent at the nursery window. As yet I had only held my daughter once. I was determined not to make that bond as there was absolutely no chance that my parents could possibly change their minds. To do that they would have to turn everything in their lives upside down.
On one of my supposedly secret visits to the nursery, I came across Midwife Compton. She was on night duty. When our paths had crossed before, it was the afternoon of my arrival and she was very friendly and helpful. This evening she seemed a bit stressed when she saw me. Perhaps in some way I used this to my advantage. When on discovering that one of the baby Girl's in the nursery had stopped breathing, was listless, and cold, I started to form a plan.My head was telling me to claim this baby as my own. That way I would be

choosing my baby's parents, instead of a Woman Almoner sitting in an office. For me this was a fight to do the right thing for my baby, to give her the best life I could. The Mother of the poor baby girl who was not breathing had been very kind to me. She had told me that she had already lost four babies. Midwife Compton stared at me as though I was some kind of witch. Then I told her of my plan. The whole time I was talking, she was desperately trying hard to revive the little mite in her hands. Eventually she laid her back in the cot and agreed to the exchange. While we were fitting new name bands on the babies' wrists I picked up my daughter and kissed her. I closed my eyes and prayed that she would have a happy and healthy life. She didn't wake on laying her back in her cot I quickly went back to my room to await the visit when I would be told my baby had died.

I snuggled under the sheet and blankets waiting for the footsteps. It didn't seem very long when the voice of Matron called my name. On turning over, she was standing in the doorway with one of the Doctor's. Matron crossed my room and put the overhead light on. She gently sat on the bed and took my hand. I had met Matron on my arrival. She had been very civil, but now sitting next to me her compassion was overwhelming. The tears for my own daughter just flowed and flowed. The Doctor recommended a sedative and Matron offered to ask my Parents to come in but all I wanted was to have something to make me sleep and get me out of this nightmare.

When I awoke the next morning my Mother was sitting by my bed. She looked tired and very sad and because of the guilt I now felt the tears started to flow again.

It was agreed that a room was to be found for my Mother so she would be at hand but instead of the normal one week stay I would be discharged the following day and recover at home.

My promise to Midwife Compton was that Baby Cooper would have a fitting funeral, and this is all I can remember saying to the staff and my Mother. It was explained to me that when she had been born she was considered to be healthy so a post-mortem was going to take place, by which time my own physical recovery would have started, and then it would be the right time to make the arrangements for her funeral.

The other Mothers on the ward were kept away from my room and so I never saw my Daughter's new Mother again.

I seemed to turn a corner with my parents. Their own grief was so great. At my lowest points I wanted to shout out that my baby was alive but deep down I knew that could never ever happen.

Living With The Consequences

Two weeks after my return to my home our GP
visited with the results from the post-mortem.
She apparently had been born with a heart
defect which would have been unlikely to be
detected on her birth. The fact she had survived
the birth had been a miracle in itself.
Having already decided that her name was to be
Verity, which means truth, I chose this as her
name, as I had been truthful to midwife
Compton. Her birth and death were registered
by my Father. The secret of my own baby's
Father's identity was to remain a secret, so a
blank box for Father was left on the birth
certificate. Her surname was to be the same as
mine, Sowersby-Smyth.

Once I had her death certificate my Parents sat
with me and it was agreed by all three of us that
she would be buried in our village church.
Up until now no one in our village had any idea
what had been going on. When I returned home
from the Hospital my parents had let it be
known that I was making a full recovery from
Glandular fever, but how could we attend a
funeral for a baby a quarter of a mile from our
home when she would be named on her
gravestone with our family name?
It came to me that maybe it would be possible
to give her, her birth Father's surname. No one
in the village would be suspicious, especially if

we held her funeral early in the morning. For me I would be laying her to rest with her correct identity.

Father looked into it and it wasn't a problem. Anyone can be buried under an alias (as they thought) as long as it wasn't done for fraudulent purposes. Well it certainly wasn't that. I could see my parents were pleased at my suggestion, it meant that 'Verity Constance (after my Aunt) Cooper's grave could be attended by all of us and a suitable story told and no one would be the wiser.

Father agreed early morning would be appropriate and when he made arrangements with our Vicar, he told him not to worry about the funding for the church porch, he would see to it that funding would be there. The vicar was onside. Verity's funeral was to take place the following week on the Friday. Father made all the arrangement, all I had to do was to choose my flowers.

When I was a small child it had been most enjoyable to have been asked to be bridesmaid four times. Each time a posy of blooms was given to me to carry. Each time they were different flowers and different colours but they were always so pretty. This is what I had in mind for Verity.

The feeling of loss was huge but of course it wasn't possible to discuss it with anyone. The week dragged by and then on the Thursday afternoon my brother arrived. Mother hadn't said anything about Richard coming home, apparently he wasn't sure that he would be able to make it. He was on a two year secondment in New York.

The following morning I woke early to hear the birds singing and the sun shining. I couldn't face any breakfast but managed a cup of tea. We drove the quarter of a mile in Father's car and the Rev Hill was waiting for us at the door. We walked into the church and it took my breath away to see, placed on a trestle, the little white coffin belonging to Verity.

It wasn't a very long service. What was there to say? After all she had had no life, but our Vicar was able to make it personal and moving. The whole congregation was made up of our family of four, the Vicar's wife, and the two funeral directors.

When the service was over, the younger of the two funeral directors gently lifted the coffin and carried it out as we followed.

The plot had been selected with great care by my Father. It was on the perimeter of the graveyard under the branches of a beautiful oak tree, overlooking the fields of Hertfordshire. The sun was so bright and shone directly on her coffin as it was lowered into its final resting place.

The flowers were all laid to the front. Mother and Father's, Richard's, Aunt Constance's, a tribute sent from St.Agnes's, mine and a smaller posy which had no card.

When looking back now it all seemed to happen so fast. One minute I was arriving at the Hospital awaiting the birth of my baby, the next, Verity's funeral had taken place and Mother and Father were asking what I would like to do (with my life)? It's a shame that conversation hadn't taken place before my drives with Derek!

Richard stayed a week before he flew back to New York, and in that time we went on numerous walks. We spoke about his life in America and that he was feeling it harder to come back to England as he was making his life out there. He still had six months of his secondment left but planned to fly over again in the summer to let our parents know of his future plans. He tried to help me sort out my plans for the future. After all it was still possible for me to go to University and he offered to speak to Mother and Father for me. Too much had happened now and I felt the need to recover mentally and physically. At the moment, my plans involved Aunt Constance and the need to go back to the little nest I had made with her. The only thing stopping me was looking after Verity's grave.

On Richard's last day we went to the grave yard. The flowers at her grave had already perished and had been removed so we both took with us fresh flowers. We didn't stay long. The weather had deteriorated and we were going through a chilly spell but Richard had spoken to our parents for me and Mother had readily agreed to visit her Grand daughter's grave and replace the flowers. It was then he asked who Verity's Father was. I wasn't sure if he had been asked to find out, but I told him in no uncertain terms that I would never tell.

Early the following morning Richard's, taxi arrived. The three of us waved him goodbye and my life started to feel empty again.

After breakfast I broached the subject with my parents about my having a return visit to Aunt Constance's. They showed no objection and the following week my Mother and I were on our way again to Kings Lynn.

It was lovely being back with Aunt Constance. She didn't fuss but still managed to make me feel at home. Once my Mother had left and we were on our own, I thanked her for all her help on my previous stay and she was quite touched to think that she had been so supportive.

It was while we were on a shopping trip to Kings Lynn that the subject of libraries came up and that all the villages on the outskirts of Kings Lynn had no access to a library. That was the seed that I needed. Having passed my driving test at school, something every girl was encouraged to do, and having a genuine interest in literature (that would have been my subject of choice at University), would it be possible to set up some kind of mobile library? Aunt Constance had such a large network of friends who seemed to know everyone, and it wasn't long before I was talking to the local councillors about my suggestions. If they had any doubts that a nineteen year old could organise such a project no one showed any sign. The past year's experience had made me grow up, and fast.

After three months it was agreed. The council would buy and provide an equipped van suitable for viewing books and pay all running costs. The books would be chosen by myself and the librarians in the main library in Kings Lynn. By this time I had a lot of contact with the team of four. The books were to be partly paid for by the council and partly donations from all of Aunt Constance's friends. My job would be to visit the villages on given days and scheduled times for adults. Then on three mornings a week, to visit schools on a rota and encourage reading, either by listening to the children individually or to read to them. This would have to be unpaid, voluntary work. However this wasn't a problem as Father now gave me a suitable allowance.

How I loved my job. Driving around country lanes, then stopping and meeting so many lovely people. The bonus of course was visiting the schools. I couldn't have been happier. Every month I would return home to my parents so as to keep my word and visit Verity's grave. Six months after her funeral, her grave stone was put in place. The engraving was quite simple.

Verity Constance Cooper
Whose short life touched
Our Hearts Forever
8th April 1960 to   9th April 1960

It brought back all the pain of her and the baby I gave birth to. By this time Verity to me, had become my daughter, and the feeling was so strong that it broke my heart again so see it engraved in stone. Had it not been that on the Monday I had to be back in Kings Lynn for the mobile library, my resolve for the second time would have been broken.

By this time my parents were not only giving me a good allowance, but had bought me a brand new mini to make my week- ends travelling home far easier.

Life carried on like this for another year. I enjoyed the routine of my job but of course every day was different, seeing and meeting new people. Then one day I was parked in a village, outside the school gates. When looking up the road to the Church hall I noticed a blood donor vehicle. There was a while before the children's story time, so I decided to make enquires and do my good deed for the community.

On entering the church hall, a line of beds and screens had been set up and a couple of villagers were already filling in a questionnaire. Behind me a very commanding female voice asked if she could be of assistance. I explained that I had never donated blood before but was willing to do so. She looked pleased and said it wouldn't take too long and there was a cup of tea and a biscuit after. Not forgetting my library duty, it was arranged that I would go back at the end of the school day.

At quarter to four I made my way back up to the church hall. It wasn't as busy so the nurse made herself comfortable at the side of my bed where she proceeded to take my details. My name, address, age and then blood group. The nurse's face lit up. She couldn't believe what I had said and called one of her colleagues over.

Apparently my blood group is quite rare and they had been told that morning that a child was laying dangerously ill in Norwich hospital due to being run over. The blood donor units had all been made aware of this and should they be lucky enough to have a donor with this blood group then they had to let the hospital know immediately!

The nurse proceeded to take my blood, and her colleague went to the vicarage to use their phone and let the hospital know. They informed her that my blood would be collected by a hospital driver.

Within twenty minutes the driver arrived. Once it had been packed into a special travel box the driver left and I was given a cup of tea and biscuit.

It was really only after telling Aunt Constance of my day that the enormity of my being a blood donor hit me, and what it would mean to this child. In my mind was my own daughter. She was out there, and although being too young to be crossing the road alone now, what if she were ever in this situation?

Within two weeks, I knew in my heart that I needed to be living in Hertfordshire near Verity's grave, and possibly not too far away from my own daughter.

Aunt Constance understood my dilemma regarding Verity and reluctantly, as she had grown used to my company, helped me with the task of packing my belongings.

The Council were not so happy to hear of my decision and made it quite clear that a lot of adults and children were being let down. Once it was made clear to them that I wouldn't abandon the library until a suitable replacement could be found, they were only too happy to help.

In the end it took four months before the keys were handed over to my replacements. The problem was that the Council still insisted that they were unable to pay a salary, therefore the job had to be taken on a voluntary basis.
The best way in the end was to have two volunteers and let them sort out the hours between them. It fell to me to give them some form of introduction to the job and its clients, and as I got to know them both I was happy with the choice that had been made.

In the four months during the transition time, my parents had never asked what next or what had I planned to do with myself. Sitting at the dining table the first morning after moving back to Ashgreen and enjoying a lazy breakfast my Father lowered his paper, looked at me and asked,
"Caroline, your Mother and I want you to know that it is lovely to have you back home.
However, we have been wondering as to whether you have any idea what you would like to do?"
With this Mother broke in,
"Caroline, you know it isn't too late to be a debutante".
I must have looked horrified because Mother started to stutter,

"If it is ok with the both of you then I would like to have a couple of weeks to myself. When I was at Aunt Constance's I never took any time off, only Bank holidays and such like. By the end of that time I think things will seem clearer and I can think through all of my options".

Father was nodding." Quite right Caroline, if you need any help you know where we are. Perhaps if we say two weeks, then we can go from there".

"Sounds perfect, thank you, both of you for being so understanding".

That was how it was left.

In the two weeks I visited Verity every day, not always taking flowers, but just because for some reason it seemed to give me some form of peace being in the graveyard, and it gave me time to reflect on the course of action I had taken in the last 22 months.

After having so much freedom at Aunt Constance's it was a struggle to be back under the family roof. Father gave me a very good allowance which was great to live on, but wouldn't have allowed me to buy a property. Of course there was always the option of renting, but where? After spending time at Verity's grave side I would get into my mini and drive. There were little towns and villages all within 15 miles of home that I had never even heard of before. Most had a tearoom, where I would have my lunch. If there was an estate agent then I would peruse their window trying to find a possible nest for myself. It's strange because in that time a job or career never entered my head. It seemed to me a foregone conclusion that starting up another mobile library was what I wanted to do.

Two weeks passed and as my Father had scheduled we had our family meeting. While the three of us were sitting in my Father's study it crossed my mind how much he had mellowed towards me since the birth of my daughter. My Mother went at least twice a week to Verity's grave and changed the flowers. I began to wonder if in time before leaving the maternity hospital would they possibly have changed their minds and allowed me to bring their rightful Granddaughter home?

Much to my delight they had realised that living back at home was probably a bit stifling for me and so told me about the trust fund that had been set up for me by my Paternal Grandfather. My Grandfather had died six months after I was born and as a girl it never occurred to me that I would have inherited anything. It turned out that there was enough for me to buy either a flat or a cottage size house. Instantly there was so much for me to think about and when I told them my plans for hopefully starting another mobile library, they were genuinely happy for me.

The next day, I made contact with the county council to see if they were receptive of my idea. An appointment was made for the following Friday which gave me three days to organise my presentation. In some ways, this was going to be harder than Kings Lynn as I didn't have the support of Auntie and her friends in the know. Wanting to really do this on my own, I turned down the offer from my Father to have a word with some of his contacts.

 Friday couldn't come quick enough, how the meeting went would be a big factor in where I was going to purchase my first home.

Setting out far too early and having to wait outside the Council Chambers for nearly an hour did nothing to calm my nerves. Eventually, my name was called and I felt as though I was going on the stage for a first night.

The meeting went as well as could be expected. There had been no definite 'yes' but they were impressed with my knowledge of the out laying villages and schools who could possibly benefit. The fact that it would be run on a voluntary basis they liked as well. I had also managed to get a break down of vehicle costs and furbishment of books from Kings Lynn Council. They even offered to supply me with feedback from the local community benefitting from the scheme. All I had to do now was wait for two weeks until the Councillors sat for their next meeting. I realised that there was a lot riding on this, as I never considered a back up plan. Success! the Council were happy with my application. They had already made contact with the council in Kings Lynn. The education department were compiling a list of schools that would benefit from the library and supported reading, the only stipulation was that they would like the mobile library returned at the end of each day. When staying with Auntie I garaged it in the unused stable block but that didn't matter, I would just drive to the council depot each day.

While waiting for delivery of my new van, I spent each day trawling the estate agents in earnest for my new home. It didn't take very long. In Brook Norton, the nearest town to my parents, a river ran on the outskirts. Originally some cottages had been built that ran along the bank but since the war they had been left empty and had become derelict. They, and the surrounding land, had been sold, and planning permission had been sought to replace them, like for like. The new row of eight cottages looked old on the outside, but had modern features on the inside, ideal for a young person. They had two bedrooms and a bathroom upstairs. Downstairs consisted of a kitchen and combined dining area, and a snug lounge. They had just come onto the market. The first one had been finished and was being used as a show house. I fell in love with the cottage outside and in straight away, but preferred its adjoining neighbour as it had a bigger garden and small attached garage. The estate agent pointed out that as builders were still working on it, entry was not allowed, but that didn't matter, I had chosen my new home. Back at the Estate agents, I paid a deposit and then hurriedly drove back home to tell my parents my exciting news.

Within three months, I had moved into my new home. My garden faced south, and when my parents came to view my new home they both thought the addition of a little conservatory would be ideal to capture the sun on chillier days.

The remaining six cottages still had builders in them, so I approached the foreman for some advice. Instantly he agreed with my parents suggestion, and thought the best way forward would be if the Architect who designed the cottages could come and make some recommendations.

My library was now up and running and was proving to be even more successful than in Norfolk. I made arrangements for the foreman and architect to come by late the following Monday afternoon.

That Monday, I had a visit into one of the village schools, so I parked up in the playground just after the children had returned to school after lunch. Then, I hurriedly ran up the road to a family run bakers, to buy some cakes. I wanted to make my cottage look homely and get on the good side of the architect! Father had said that some professionals think they know best, and he might be offended at my suggestion of a conservatory.

I had no need to worry, Ted, the foreman, had been watching for my return. Within five minutes there was a knock at my door and Ted introduced me to, David, the architect. He was much younger than Ted. Looking about thirty five, tall and slim with light brown hair and a smiley face. Inviting them both in, Ted apologised, as he had to supervise a late delivery of materials, and off he went.

It's strange but at no time did I feel awkward with David. After my only experience with a man, Derek, I had become a little aloof in male company.

He seemed genuinely pleased with my choice of furnishings and congratulated me on making my cottage a home. We went into the garden and looked back to the rear of my little home and I explained what I had in mind. He immediately could see the benefits, and asked if he could take a few measurements. While he was doing that I made a pot of tea, and laid my selection of cakes out.

It was so pleasant talking to someone who was so passionate about their work. Two hours later, he jumped up. It was then that he told me he was a widower he had lost his wife in a car crash, and that he had to collect his daughter from his parents and, as soon as he had some quotes he would get in contact. With that, he was out the door and running up the road to his car.

From then on, David visited my cottage at least twice a week with plans and quotes. Then, once the build of my conservatory had started it was even more frequent. Looking back, I think the builders gave him a little leg pulling, but it didn't seem to bother him. On one of David's drop in's he had told me that on another site he was working on, one of the carpenters had badly cut his hand. He seemed quite shocked after seeing the amount of blood the carpenter had lost. This led to him telling me that his daughter had needed a transfusion, when she had been travelling in the car when his wife was killed. I told him of my experience with a child who had been run over and my donation. As he couldn't say thank you to the donor of his daughter, he asked, could he make a gesture and thank me for the child who received my blood by taking me out to dinner? He caught me unaware, but he seemed so genuine that I agreed, but insisted that I would meet him there. I still didn't feel confident enough to be in a car with a man on my own.

The dinner was delightful, everything a young girl imagines a date is going to be. We laughed, talked easily. As the evening wore on he told me how much his daughter meant to him and that after his wife had died, it was his daughter that got him through the dark days that followed. It was then that he confided that his Mother (who was baby sitting that night) and his sister bought all of his daughter's clothes but he would like to buy her a dress for a party that she had been invited to and wondered would I go along for moral support? I was flattered that he valued our friendship so much. I agreed but on one condition that I met his daughter before the big event. It was agreed that he would bring Andrea to my cottage on the following Saturday for tea.

It is quite bizarre when you think I had no experience of children, and yet I was prepared had I been allowed to bring my own daughter up. As it was, I didn't even know what children liked to eat.

The next day my library was at the local primary school, and during afternoon playtime I spoke to the head teacher regarding this very subject. She had two children of her own and although they were nearly my age she was very helpful on what most children enjoyed.

By Saturday afternoon, I had become a little nervous. I realised that it was important to me that Andrea liked me. The table was set and the kettle ready to be boiled, when I heard David's car draw up. I heard them walking up my garden path, and the door knocker rapped at the door. With a smile on my face I opened the door.

For some reason I was expecting Andrea to be about 8 years old. Instead, David was holding the hand of a much younger child. She was about 3, and she was shyly looking down at the floor. Then she looked up and I was totally unprepared.

Chapter Eighteen

Two days after Harold had contacted the back numbers at the Times newspaper, there was a heavy thud on the hall floor. Harold and his wife were sitting having their breakfast in the kitchen. Harold looked up from his newspaper. "That sounds as though that is something for me".

He was up out of his chair. Edna knew from old that Harold would be totally consumed with the job that he had taken on. It was reminiscent of his years in the Metropolitan police.

He walked back into the kitchen with his parcel under his arm.

"If you need me, I shall be in the study, we didn't have anything pressing for today did we?"

Edna smiled up at him. "You did say that you were going to give the lawn a once over, but it isn't in real need. Actually I might defrost the freezer".

"Good idea!"

With that, he picked his cup of tea up and disappeared into his study.

When he opened up the bundle, there was a compliment slip and a scribbled note on the bottom from John, at the Times back numbers.

It made my day hearing from you again. If you need anymore information, don't hesitate to call
All the best,
John

Harold put the note to one side and unrolled the papers. There were three in all, and Harold was hoping that there must be some useful information in one of them.
They were rolled up in date order. The first had the announcement of the Judge's death. Harold checked the date. As he had assumed correctly, it was two days after they had set out on their holiday to Australia. The second paper had printed an article giving an in-depth insight into the Judge's career but started with the details of his funeral. This had been attended by his widow, Lady Sowersby-Smyth, their son, who resides in New York, and daughter. The family would like to thank friends and associates for their condolences, and hope they can join them for the memorial service to be held in St. Albans Cathedral on Friday, 25th February at 2pm. Harold moved on to the final paper. There again, the funeral was mentioned, and this time the location was given. The parish church of St.

Andrews, Ashgreen, where Sir Sowersby-Smyth lived on the family estate. It also went on to state that, the memorial service had been very well attended, and listed some of the prestigious members of the bar and Politicians that had been seen. Underneath, a photo had been printed of the family Lady Sowersby-Smith, her daughter, and husband. Harold was pleased to see that it mentioned Caroline's husband. He felt sure that this piece of news would please Evelyn Compton.

He picked his pencil up that was lying on the desk next to the telephone and pad, and started tapping it on the desk. This was his normal habit while thinking out his next move.
Ten minutes later, he was walking back into the kitchen where he could hear his wife washing up,
"Edna, probably a bit short notice, but I was thinking of having a drive over to Maud and George's in Biggleswade. Would you like to come with me, and I could drop you off and do my bit of business then, come back after and Perhaps we could have a fish and chip supper with them?"
Edna liked this idea. She had been planning to suggest a visit over to see her sister. Her sister was just as a keen knitter as she was, and Edna could take over the patterns her sister was

waiting for instead of having the bother of putting them in the post.

"Excellent idea, I will go and ring her now, what day shall I suggest?"

Harold was keen now to move on with his enquiries, "Any day will suit me, the sooner the better".

With that, Edna went to the hall to phone. Within minutes she was back,

"That was lucky Maud was just about to walk out the door, market day. I suggested tomorrow afternoon. She said that would work well as George was playing golf, and we could have a good chat, and fish and chips would be lovely".

Harold raised his eyebrow, he knew what his sister in law's idea of a good chat was. No wonder George spent so much of his time on the golf course.

Chapter Nineteen

The following day was a beautiful May Day.
Harold decided to mow the lawn in the
morning. He wanted to give himself something
physical to do. The worst thing for Harold was
to over think the next stage of his commission.
After an early lunch, Harold and Edna set out on
the two hour drive to Biggleswade. On their
arrival Edna got out of the car with a basket full
of patterns, wool and her current knitting
project. Harold waited for her to ring the door
bell, and within seconds the door was opened
by Maud. Harold waved out to her and drove
off. The village he was heading for was only
twenty minutes away, and it proved to be a
very pleasant drive. After five minutes, he was
driving down pretty country lanes.
Having never been to the village before, he
didn't know where the village church was
located, but seeing a petrol garage just before
he reached the Main Street he thought he
would top up with petrol and ask.
It wasn't long before he was back in the car and
with directions for St. Andrews. Two minutes
later, the church was on his right hand side. He
pulled onto the small gravel car park, and got

out of his car. Unaware that someone was walking towards him pushing a bike, a voice called to him.

"Good afternoon, can I be of some help?" Harold looked to his right where the voice was coming from, but had to shield his eyes as the sun was shining into them.

"Hello", Harold replied. By now, the figure of a man was only a couple of feet away, with an arm outstretched ready to shake Harold's hand.

"Yes, hello, I am the vicar of this parish Reverend Hill, how can I help?"

"Hello Vicar, I am Harold Brownlow. An old acquaintance informed me the other day that one of your local residents had passed away just over a year ago. Sir Sowersby- Smyth, although I new him as Judge Sowersby-Smyth. I thought as I was over this way it would be a good opportunity to pay my respects".

"Yes quite, I see, a very respected member of the community. I take it that you are possibly a policeman or perhaps even a retired policeman? "

Harold, laughing, went on to say." Yes I am retired, and that is how my wife and I missed the announcement in the paper! We decided to have a four month trip out to Australia to see family and sight see. I understand there was a memorial service for him in St. Albans Cathedral?"

"Yes there was, and very well attended. I did over hear possibly two of your former colleagues speaking after the service. They were commenting in the back row of the church on it being a 'who's who' or I think one called it, 'a rogues gallery' It made me think later, for such a big turnout of both sides of our judicial system, the judge must have been a fare man".
"A fair man is a good description".

Harold didn't want to be rude to the Vicar, but he had the impression that he would have been happy to stand and talk all afternoon. Whereas Harold, needed to move the conversation on if he was going to forward his investigation.
"Vicar, I hope I am not holding you up?"
The Reverend Hill looked down at his watch.
"Well, actually I hope you won't consider me rude but I do have parishioners to look in on this afternoon, but would you like me to just show you where Sir Sowersby-Smyth has been laid to rest?"
"I would be extremely grateful, thank you".
With that, the Reverend Hill led the way into the graveyard, passing through a small wooden gate and under a small porch.
The Vicar continued. "Sir Sowersby-Smyth and his family have always been most generous. The porch we have just walked under was donated, um, let me think, yes, eighteen years ago now. Did you know that the family reside next door from here?"

Not waiting for Harold to answer, the Vicar
continued.

"When I say the family, I mean Lady Sowersby-
Smyth. Their son lives in America, and has done
for a number of years but, what I think is
extremely nice, is that the daughter Caroline
and her husband are going to take on the family
house. It's very unusual for the daughter of the
house and not the son. Anyway, Lady Sowersby-
Smyth had decided she no longer wanted to live
in the house, so the son in law, who is an
architect, has designed a house for her in the
grounds. By all accounts it is very nearly
finished. Were you thinking of paying the family
a visit? There is usually someone there this time
of the day, and I think that all of the
condolences they have received it has helped
them come to terms with their grief. Here we
are".

Both men stopped in front of a newly engraved
gravestone. Harold could see that it was indeed,
Judge Sowersby-Smyth's, and that this was a
family area as both his parents gravestones
were directly in front of his own.

Harold, not slow to capitalise on an opportunity
replied.

"I might just do that. Where exactly is their
property?"

"That's good, I feel sure they would be pleased
to see you. The house sits at the bottom of a
fairly long drive, so I would suggest you go in

your car. Turn right onto the road, and then turn right into the first drive you see on the right. As I say, you will drive for about half a mile before you see the house, but the gardens are beautiful".

He looked at his watch.

"Very nice to meet you, I will leave you in peace now, good afternoon".

"Good afternoon to you, Vicar". They shook hands again.

Harold stayed in the graveyard for about fifteen minutes. He paid his respects, and then decided to have a walk around. The graveyard was kept immaculately. No long grass or gravestones overgrown with ivy. The setting was perfect over looking fields, none of the stones were neglected and a number even of older ones had fresh flowers on them.

Once back in his car, he gave himself some time to think. Finding the address of Caroline like this had saved him a lot work, he didn't want to jeopardise any possible interview by being impetuous.

Fifteen minutes later, Harold had taken the right turn and had just turned into the drive of the late Judge Sowesby-Smyth's home. He drove very slowly. Partly, to admire the grounds of lawns, huge rhododendron bushes and varieties of old established trees and, partly because the drive was very bendy. He still wasn't sure who he hoped to find there. His day so far had been very successful.

Yet another bend, and then the whole drive opened up to a view of a beautifully proportioned late Victorian house. Harold could see that the large front door was open, and what looked like a teenage girl struggling with a large cardboard box was coming out. He parked next to the mini which was the only car in the parking area, and got out.

As Harold was walking towards the door, he realised that he had been mistaken about the teenager. She was in fact older, but very slim, and dressed in a t-shirt and jeans with her blonde hair tied up. Could he have hit the jackpot? could this be Caroline?

The young lady was walking towards Harold. Harold spoke first." Hello, I hope I haven't called at an inconvenient moment but I have just come from St. Andrews, where I was paying my respects to Judge Sowersby-Smyth. My name is Harold Brownlow, I am a retired Chief Inspector of the Metropolitan police".

The young lady put the large box down and introduced herself.

"Hello, Mr Brownlow, I am Caroline, the Judge's daughter. I am pleased to meet you. It has been very gratifying for Mother and I to know the high esteem in which my Father was held".

She looked quite sad while she spoke, but all of a sudden, her face lit up and she continued.

"My Father always thought that there were some policemen, whom if they were not in that profession then would likely have been criminals themselves. Mr Brownlow, my Father never spoke about any cases he'd sat on, but occasionally he may make a remark about the investigating officers, and I can say that he had the greatest respect for you".

Harold was very surprised at this remark, and was genuinely taken aback.

"Well that is very kind of you to say so, but please call me Harold as Mr Brownlow makes me feel rather ancient. It was the Vicar who enlightened me with your Mother's address".

Caroline bent down and picked up her box again. Harold sensed that she was in a hurry, which was a shame because he still needed to bring up the question of Midwife Compton.

"Harold, I am sorry but would you mind if I carried on loading my car? It's just that the village is having a jumble sale tomorrow in the church hall, and the WI ladies who run it would like all contributions of jumble to be delivered by three – thirty, and I have another car load after this".

"How it would be if I was to load my car as well, would that help? Paying my respects to your Father wasn't the only thing I wanted to speak to you about".

Too late, he had said it. She was looking at him now in a very intense way, had he completely blown any chance of Mrs Compton's issue being resolved?

"The offer of helping with the jumble is most welcome, but first can you give me a clue as to what you wanted to speak to me about?"

Harold looked at Caroline, and spoke.

"Midwife Evelyn Compton, she wants to know that you are ok".

"Yes, I'm very happy, but is she alright? I have often thought about her. She must be quite elderly now".

Harold instantly felt more relaxed, he now knew that Caroline was a nice and sincere person.

"She is elderly and a few months back had a health scare, but is fine now. Look shall we deliver your jumble, then, perhaps I could take you for tea somewhere?"

Caroline smiled back," I have a much better idea we will deliver all of this, and then come back here and I will do tea and cake, and answer any questions you have for me, and you can tell me all about Midwife Compton".

With Harold helping it didn't take long to finish loading Caroline's car, and with the rest put into Harold's they set off.

When they reached the church hall, the WI ladies reminded Harold of his days in the army. He could see quite clearly why Caroline was keen to arrive before 3.30pm. With the cars unloaded they headed back.

Caroline showed Harold the down stairs cloakroom, and then made her way to the back of the house where the huge kitchen lay. He could hear where she was by the clattering of cups, saucers and plates, and the whistle of a kettle.

Joining her in the kitchen, he asked if he could be of any assistance.

"Everything is under control, but if you could bring the cake? I thought we would sit in the conservatory".

Once they were both sitting down and Caroline had poured the tea and offered Harold a slice of cake, Harold thought it best if he started to explain.

"A lot of policemen, when they retire at 55 feel the need to carry on working for a few more years. I was no exception. I felt I still had a few more years left in me. A good friend of mine introduced me to a local Solicitor. Solicitors sometimes need some, shall we say, low stakes investigating. That went very well, and then my wife and I decided to move to Sussex and, by luck, I was introduced to another Chamber of Solicitors who had exactly the same needs. One of the senior Solicitors of this practice is Evelyn Compton's daughter".

Harold felt his throat was getting a bit dry so he drank his tea. Caroline immediately offered him another cup, which he accepted.

"Right, so that is how I met Mrs Compton. What she asked me to do, was to try and find you. I have no idea why, that is your business, but I perceived that she was very anxious to find you and, if you were in complete agreement, she would very much like to see you".

Caroline put her cup and saucer down.

"I have hoped that one day she would come looking for me. I over the years, as I said, have often wondered about her. She was extremely kind to me, and at a huge risk to herself. Please go back to her and let her know that I am married with a daughter. My husband, David, is an architect and, within months of my Father passing away, my Mother had decided that she would like us to come and move in with her. Our house is only twenty minutes away, but now a days Mother has no living in staff, and as you can see it is rather big for one person. Actually it's rather big for us three, but Mother didn't want to sell up so David has drawn up plans and an annexe is being built to the back of the house. My brother lives in America and is more than happy for us to be here, so as you can see by the amount of boxes this afternoon I am slowly working my way through the house sorting it out for when we move in. Mother, other than her bedroom furniture and desk, wants all new so it has become a mammoth task! The fortunate thing there is no deadline, and I can take my time".

With that she smiled at Harold.

Harold replied."My day couldn't have gone any better. If it is alright with you I will get back to Mrs Compton and let her know that you would like to see her again. As I said, I have no idea of your business, but I do have to ask, does your husband know?"

"There are no worries on that score. David and I have no secrets".

Harold smiled." In my experience, that is a recipe for a good marriage. Now how would you like to proceed regarding making arrangements? If you like, I can pass on your address and telephone number and Mrs Compton can make contact, or would you prefer to do it?"

Caroline had already stood up and was making her way back into the main house. "I'll write my details down for you, and then Mrs Compton can decide".

On her return, Caroline handed Harold her details but, looking a bit pensive she asked. "You don't think she will change her mind do you? We do have a lot to catch up on".

"When I met her, she seemed to me to be the type of person that, when she makes a decision she sticks to it. Now, I have probably taken a lot of your time this afternoon. Thank you for tea, the cake was very nice but, I am due to be back to rescue my brother in law from my sister in law's constant chatter! ".

Caroline, feeling relaxed, again laughed." That sounds nice, are you going to eat with them?" "Yes, a fish and chip supper, my wife's favourite, so I will say goodbye and, if for what ever reason you have a change of heart, then I have left my card on the tea tray for you. I won't telephone Mrs Compton's daughter until tomorrow afternoon".

Harold got in his car and turned it around. Then, waving to Caroline, who was already waving back, drove away.

" Well that went very well. I wonder what she meant by 'a lot to catch up on?" With a smile on his face he joined the road at the end of the drive, and made his way back to his family for his supper.

Chapter Twenty

Keeping his word, Harold didn't phone Veronica Cousins until 4pm the following day. He thought he would try ringing her at her office first, so that it would give her the opportunity to visit her Mother on her way home with the news Evelyn Compton had been hoping for. Harold went to his study to make his call.

"Good afternoon, Wallace, Featherby and Cousin's, how may I help".

"Good afternoon this is Harold Brownlow would it be possible to speak to Mrs Cousins?"

"If you would like to hold the line I will see if she is available".

Veronica Cousins voice came on the line.

"Mr Brownlow, I wasn't expecting to hear from you so soon. I do hope everything is alright?"

"Mrs Cousins, my investigation couldn't have gone better. Now would you like me to come in and see you, or are you available now?"

Harold thought he already knew the answer to this as she sounded very impatient for the news.

"I am available now, before I contacted you my Mother did tell me the whole story and I can understand her concerns and worries".

Harold gave a little cough to clear his throat, a little ritual he used to do before giving evidence in court and then proceeded to tell Veronica his findings.

"Well, it is all good news. I found Caroline quite quickly, and what made it easier sadly, was the death of her Father. Sowersby-Smyth is a very unusual name, which makes investigating a lot easier. Please tell your Mother that she is extremely happy. She is married with one daughter and currently moving back into her old family home, where an annexe is being built by her architect husband, in the grounds, for her Mother. She is a very nice young lady, and was greatly concerned about your Mother and said that she had always thought, and I think hoped that your Mother would look for her. Of course, not knowing the background history, I did ask her if this was a secret that she had kept from her husband, and she let me know that they have no secrets. Most importantly, she would really like to see your Mother again, as she said, I quote,' we do have a lot to catch up on'. I did not mention that your Mother wanted to locate a grave. I think that would be better to come from her, when she thinks the time is right. Now, regarding a meeting, I have her address and telephone number and she is happy for your Mother to decide where, when and who contacts who. I do hope this news is very satisfactory".

"Mr Brownlow, you have no idea how pleased I am to hear from you with such good news! In fact, I think it is a good time for me to finish here for the day and make my way to my Mother's to give her the good news. I know she will be so pleased. Now, I would really like to ask your advice on how we should proceed, after all I have never met her and my Mother hasn't seen her for eighteen years".

"I think the best course of action would be perhaps if you were to ring her yourself. It sounds as though it might be too emotional for your Mother. I am assuming you will be present when they meet, so you can make any arrangements that will suit you. My only advice would be that if at any stage of the meeting there is possibility of high emotions, then perhaps meet in one of your homes instead of a public place. That way no embarrassment needs to be caused".

"Yes Mr Brownlow, that sounds like very good advice. Now, something which we never discussed was your fees, so perhaps you can let me have the invoice and perhaps could you send it to my home address?"

"Mrs Cousins don't think about that, now all I would ask is that you let me know how it ends up, and then perhaps we will discuss it. If when you see your Mother, something crops up that I have forgotten to mention, then please ring me I will be at home all evening. Good bye".

Veronica replied with the same courtesy." Good bye Mr Brownlow and thank you from myself and my Mother".

Chapter Twenty One

Veronica hurriedly tidied her desk and was thankful that she had nothing urgently pending in her IN tray. Picking up her handbag, briefcase and jacket, she popped her head into her secretary's office.

"Margaret, I have to go and see my Mother, so I won't be coming back into the office again today. Tomorrow, I will aim to be here for 8am, if there is anything outstanding you wish me to see can you leave it in on my desk. See you tomorrow, goodbye".

Before Margaret had a chance to reply, Veronica was already gone, and she could hear the outer door of the reception area being opened, then closed.

"Goodnight Mrs Cousin's". Margaret called after her.

Veronica arrived at the Willow's at a quarter to five. Parking her car, she hurried across the car park. Just as she got to the entrance door, the Manager of the home was coming out she was pleased to see Veronica.

"Hello, was it me you have come to see?"

Veronica hurried passed. She had no intention of slowing her pace, she knew from experience that to stop and exchange the time of day with Yvonne Kelly would waste valuable time with her Mother.

"Hello Yvonne, no not today, wanted to see Mother, Goodbye".

Veronica went straight to the reception desk to sign in the visitors book. When she turned around, her Mother was standing behind her.

"Hello Mum, I didn't hear you".

"Hello dear. Well I was just going to my room before supper, and I thought I heard your voice. It's lovely to see you, but I wasn't expecting you. Everything is alright, isn't it?"

Veronica smiled at her Mother.

"Everything is perfect, come on, let's go to your room".

Veronica took her Mother's arm and they headed for Evelyn's room.

When they entered, Veronica drew her over to the two arm chairs in the window, and they both sat down. By this time, Veronica was practically bursting to tell her Mother the news, and became a little sharp when her Mother spoke.

"Would you like a drink dear?"

"No thank you Mum, listen, forget about all of that, Harold Brownlow has just phoned me. He has found Caroline, and he has spoken with her and she would really like to see you and, what's more, she has thought about you often in the time since St.Agnes".

Evelyn was finding it hard to keep up. Veronica had been speaking so fast, and the magnitude of the news seemed to overwhelm her, and before she could answer she had burst into tears.

Veronica got up and went to the bedside cabinet where her Mother always had a box of paper hankies. She picked the box up, and knelt in front of her Mother offering it to her. Evelyn took one, and started to dab her eyes.

Veronica spoke," Its good news isn't it, Mum. I am so pleased, because Harold said that she is a very nice young lady, and I think after seeing her, you will finally be able to accept what happened".

"Is that what Mr Brownlow said, that she was nice?"

"Yes he did. He also said that she is married with one daughter, and that she and her husband have no secrets, so meeting her will not put her in a compromising position.He has also given me her address and phone number and said it is entirely up to you as to how you make contact with her, so, we really have got to make some plans. He seems to think that when you meet, it is probably best not to do it in a public place as you won't really have any privacy. I am quite happy for you to meet at my house, or if you prefer, we can go to her home? She lives in a small village in Hertfordshire, and is in the process of moving her family back into the family home".

Evelyn had now composed herself.

"Could we go to see her? It would mean a lot of driving for you, but I do so want to see where she lives and that she really is truly happy".

"Mum, I will do whatever it takes for you to be able to put this behind you. I will phone Caroline tomorrow and make plans. Is that ok, are you happy with that?"

"Yes, I think that would be perfect, thank you".

Chapter Twenty Two

The following day, Veronica arrived at her office for 8.00am. She wanted to make sure that as much work as possible could be cleared before she made her phone call. As always, when she walked into her office, her Clients files were lined up in priority, with attached notes. Her secretary, Margaret, was very methodical and tidy, but just a little too chatty.

She took her jacket off, and made herself comfortable at her desk. If she concentrated, she had 45 minutes ahead of her secretary with no interruptions, and she could make quite a dent in her work.

At 8.55am, Veronica looked at the clock. She had thought the best time to phone would be about 9am, but she didn't want any interruptions as she felt quite nervous at making this phone call. She didn't want to appear over bearing? But she knew that her manner, even in private, was very forthright. She scribbled a note to her secretary, saying she wasn't to be disturbed, and quickly placed it on Margaret's desk, and then returned to her office.

The phone rang only three times when a clear and crisp voice answered from the other end.

"Hello, can I help?"

"Hello, Caroline?"

"Yes, that's me".

"Hello, my name is Veronica Cousins, I am phoning on behalf of my Mother, Evelyn Compton. Harold Brownlow gave me your phone number".

"Of course, I was expecting you to phone although you took me by surprise, I didn't realise it would be quite so soon". She gave a little laugh. "But really, that doesn't matter. Mr Brownlow told me your Mother hadn't been well, I hope she is alright?"

"Please, don't worry, she is fine now. I best tell you that Mother has told me your story, and had she not had this little hiccup with her health then she would never have mentioned it. She really does want to see you, I think, to put her mind at rest. If you are in agreement, she would very much like to come to you".

The phone went very quiet and Veronica was hoping that she hadn't been too forceful, she felt relieved as Caroline suddenly started to speak.

"Mrs Cousins, you don't realise what a relief it is for me! I was desperate at the time, and so many times since I have thought about your Mother, and I have wondered if that night's actions had impacted on her life. A meeting

would be good for both of us. Have you got a
diary handy, and we will make a date now".
Veronica could feel herself nodding her head.
She was warming to this young lady.
They both agreed on the following Saturday
morning. Caroline's husband would be playing
golf and her daughter, if she was in, would likely
make herself scarce. Her Mother, whose home
it still was, would still be staying with Caroline's
Aunt. Veronica would drive her Mother and
they would start out early, and aim to be at
Caroline's future home by 10.30am.

Chapter Twenty Three

The following Saturday morning, Evelyn made her way to the dining room earlier than normal for her breakfast. Not that she felt very hungry, but she knew that even a slice of toast and a cup of tea would be better than going out on an empty stomach. The vision of herself fainting in Caroline's house spurred her on. Fortunately, no one else had entered the dining room so she hastily made her way back to her room. She checked her hair and lipstick, picked up her jacket and handbag, and went to the reception area to await Veronica's arrival. She was pleased to be early as Veronica, who was never late, was herself, 20 minutes early. As soon as her car pulled in front of the Willows, Evelyn signed herself out and went to meet her daughter.

Veronica got out of her car and walked around to the passenger door.

"Hello, Mum".

She kissed Evelyn on the cheek and held the door open for her to get in.

"Mum you look very nice! Is that new your dress and jacket?"

The dress was in navy and white, with three quarter length sleeves. It had a mandarin collar in white, and four small white buttons coming down the bodice. It came as a two piece, the jacket was in navy, with a white trim and with larger white buttons.

"Yes, it is. I bought it a couple of weeks before I was ill, and today I feel so nervous I thought it would give me some confidence".

By now, Veronica was sitting back in the driver's seat.

"You do look lovely, Mum". As she spoke, she squeezed Evelyn's hand.

Throughout the journey neither of them mentioned the visit. Instead, they talked about Evelyn's son, Michael, who lived in Australia with his young family, about Veronica's twin sons who were away at boarding school, and who no one ever heard from unless they needed more pocket money , and about the Willows, where Evelyn lived. Evelyn was still one of the co- owners along with Veronica, but neither of them took an active part in the running of the home. Edward, Veronica's husband, was the company Accountant, and then they had three directors who where the active members of the board.

When Evelyn and her husband had decided to make this life changing decision of going into residential care, they had no idea how successful they would be.

Living With The Consequences

Veronica had phoned Harold Brownlow the evening before to let him know that they were meeting Caroline on the following day, and also to ask for directions, for the best way to get there.

He gave her directions in good detail and, before Evelyn and Veronica knew it, they were turning into Caroline's childhood home.

They got out of the car and couldn't help looking around at the spectacular house and grounds. Before either could speak, they heard the big oak front door opening. A very pretty, blonde, slim, young lady came to meet them. Veronica, at first, wasn't sure who she was. Surely this can't be Caroline, she doesn't look old enough, but her Mother knew instantly who she was.

"My dear, I am so happy to see you! Veronica, this is Caroline. Caroline, this is my very clever daughter Veronica, if it wasn't for her we wouldn't be here today".

Caroline shook hands with Veronica. Then Caroline, putting her arm through Evelyn's, walked them into her future home. She showed them the downstairs cloak room, and then took them straight out to the conservatory, where a table was already set with coffee cups and biscuits, waiting for their arrival.

Evelyn looked around.

"This is a truly magnificent house".

"Yes it is, make yourselves comfortable and I will fetch the coffee, and we can start to unravel the last eighteen years".

Chapter Twenty Four

Coffee was poured and Caroline started to tell her story.

"I have absolutely no regrets to what we did that night and I hope that you have none, and if you have, then I hope you will have changed your mind by time you leave.

When I was discharged from St.Agnes my parents bought me home and for the first time in my life I felt so alone".

She looked at Evelyn and realised that she had started to get emotional so Caroline got up and sat on the sofa next to her and gently placed her hands around Evelyn's.

"Please don't be sad. I am very happy now with David my husband and my daughter Andrea".

She continued," what kept me going was making sure that I did my best for baby Cooper. I called her Verity Constance and she is buried in our parish church which is on the left side of our land. Perhaps later we can go and I will show you her grave".

Evelyn nodded. "Yes please, I would very much like to pay my respects".

"Evelyn, may I call you Evelyn".

Evelyn nodded in agreement.

"A few days after I came home my G.P. came to visit me with the results of the post-mortem. Verity had a heart defect, so much so that in the report it states that it was a miracle that she survived the birth. I don't know if you remember but her Mother had already had two still born babies and two miscarriages. When I read the report it actually helped me. Getting pregnant which was so stupid of me, was going to be put right. They were the right couple to have my baby. My parents were very supportive and Verity had a proper funeral, small but dignified.

After when I had recovered from the birth I went back to Norfolk to stay with my Aunt, whom I stayed with during my pregnancy. While I was there with the help of my Aunt Constance and the County Council I started a mobile library. It was great and then one day by accident really, I gave blood. I hadn't intended to but the blood donor unit was in the village the same day as my library. I have quite a rare blood group and the nurses had heard that day that if they saw anyone with that type then they were to immediately contact Norwich hospital as a child had been run over and was dangerously ill with that blood group. It made me think about Verity and my daughter and I wanted to come home. Verity was next door but hopefully by own daughter wasn't too far away. Again my parents were very supportive and again I opened another mobile library. After a few months I wanted to move and have some independence so with an inheritance I bought a new cottage in the neighbouring village and that was how David and I met. He was the architect for the cottages. He had been married before but he had lost his first wife in a car crash so we had some kind of shared empathy.I am sorry I have been talking without coming up for air. Can I get some more coffee or perhaps tea?"

Evelyn and Veronica spoke at the same time, "coffee please".

Then Evelyn continued," I think I best pay a visit to the cloakroom before we continue".

"Yes and while I am waiting for the water to boil I will go and get the photos I have to show you of my family".

Evelyn answered." Yes I would like that very much".

This time when they sat down Caroline automatically sat with Evelyn. Caroline passed the first framed photo to her.

With a lot of emotion in her voice she said." My husband David and my daughter Andrea".

Evelyn looked at the photo then back at Caroline.

"She is the image of you, how old is she?"

Caroline looked directly at Evelyn.

" She is eighteen ".

Evelyn was looking down at the photo."No she can't be eighteen because that's".
 Her voice tailed off and she looked back at Caroline and then burst into tears.
Veronica hadn't really been keeping up with the conversation. She was patiently waiting to see the photo. Her Mother was crying and now so was Caroline.
"I am sorry what has happened, what have I missed".
Caroline turned to face Veronica. "I was just telling your Mother that my daughter Andrea was the baby we swapped eighteen years ago in St.Agnes, she is the daughter I gave birth to".
Evelyn was now laughing." I can't believe it, how did that happen ".
Caroline continued." Actually it is sad but when I told you I had given blood to a child who had been run over well somehow the nurses had been told the wrong story. The child was a baby of 15 months it was Andrea. She was travelling in the back of the car. Her Mother was driving them home after visiting her parents in Norwich. She somehow came of the road and went down a ditch and was killed instantly. Andrea slid into one of the footwells and she received life threatening injuries and needed blood transfusions. When they checked her blood group it was rare and they assumed she had got it from her Mother as her Father didn't have the same type. So unbeknown to me my

blood was being used to save my own daughter's life".

Evelyn and Veronica looked at each other in amazement. Veronica not lost for words spoke. "In all the years I have been a Solicitor I have heard of many coincidences but this has to be the best of them".

Evelyn was nodding her head but was making eye contact with Caroline encouraging her to continue.

Caroline continued, "When moving into my cottage I realised I would like a conservatory built on the back of my home. David was the architect for the cottages so I asked him to draw up the plans. We became friends. Months passed and he asked if I would go with him and his daughter shopping for a dress for a party. I agreed but said it would be best if Andrea and I met before. For some reason I thought his daughter was older. I don't know why but I thought she was about eight or nine. When we met on my doorstep I nearly passed out with shock. As you can see by the photo there is such a strong resemblance between us".

Caroline looked at her watch. "David will be home soon please stay and have some lunch with us and he can tell you the difference you and I made to his life before Sylvia died, (David's first wife). I have never told him that there were two of us that night. I was able to keep that promise to you Evelyn but he is a clever man and knows that you were at St. Agnes with me so will probably have guessed the implication but he will never speak of it. Andrea also knows that I am her true Mother. We told her when she was sixteen. She doesn't know any detail and has never asked. She obviously has no memory of Sylvia, but she had to have some explanation because of our strong likeness. Over the years so many people have remarked upon it. So is that a yes, you will stay to lunch. Unfortunately you won't be able to meet Andrea. She has gone up to town with a group of girl friends to see a show, a matinee". Evelyn and Veronica looked at each other and nodded in agreement that they would both love to stay to lunch.

Chapter Twenty Five

While Caroline was preparing lunch, Evelyn and Veronica went for a walk in the massive grounds. As they stepped through the conservatory doors to the left, they could see the house being built for Lady Sowersby-Smyth. Compared to the main house, it was much smaller but still looked as though it would have at least six bedrooms. While admiring the new build, they heard a man's voice calling them. "Hello, I am David".

Shaking them both by the hand, Evelyn had a moment of de ja vue, of course she had met him, all those years ago at St.Agnes.

"Pretty impressive, isn't it? It's such a lovely view from here.What do you think of my Mother in laws new home?" Not waiting for an answer he continued.

"I am very pleased on how it looks. For me, It was imperative that the design completed the Manor house, otherwise both houses would have been spoilt. It is almost finished now, just a few little tweaks, and then Elizabeth will be moving in. Then we start on our own project". Evelyn was interested. " Your own project? That sounds very intriguing".

With that, David looked up to see Caroline waving to them.

"That's Caroline's signal for lunch. Let's go in, I am sure you both must be hungry, and I shall tell all while we are eating. It will be nice to have a new audience, and you can give us an honest opinion of our plans".

With that, the three of them turned around and walked back to the big house.

Five minutes later, they were sitting around a dining table in the large conservatory with the sun streaming in.

Caroline had served them a bowl of asparagus soup with small croutons floating on the top. Evelyn remarked how delightful it all looked as there, placed in the middle of the table, was a large dressed salad, already for the next course. David looking admiringly at his wife as he spoke.

"As you can see, Caroline is a marvellous cook and hostess which, if everything goes to plan, is going to be essential if we are to keep this house going. When Caroline's Mother suggested that we move in, we didn't think it would work, not all living together under the same roof, but at that stage we didn't know that she meant to move into her flat in town full time".

Caroline then took over." We completely misunderstood her. You see, my brother has made a life for himself in America and has no intention of coming back to England, and unless we come to live here, it would mean selling, which Mother didn't want to do. And I wasn't very happy her living that far away from us when over the last sixteen years I have always been so near. Mother does have so many friends locally, although she could come and stay, we thought it better that she kept her own independence".

By now they had all finished their soup, and Caroline was collecting the bowls and cutlery as David continued.

"We realised straight away that to keep the house running, it needed to work for itself, so the work to the main house is to convert eight of the bedrooms into six. All to contain their own bathrooms and study areas. Downstairs, two of the lounges will be made into a conference room, and a further two will be made into a dining room and lounge. You see, my expertise in Architecture has always been the history and renovation of buildings. When I first started out, obviously I couldn't be too choosy, but my love for historical architecture never went away. The cottage that Caroline bought had to be authentic and look typical 19th century, but on the inside, modern. So, our plan is to have architecture students, here from abroad, or in the UK to come and do specialised courses in that field. Caroline and I will run the business together, and it will enable us to carry on living in this fantastic house".

By now they were eating a delicious homemade quiche, new potatoes and salad.

Veronica was greatly impressed by their plans and wished them well. As a working woman herself, she admired anyone who had the foresight to recognise an opportunity. After strawberries and cream, they made their way into one of the sitting rooms. Evelyn felt full, and hoped that she wouldn't disgrace herself by falling asleep because she was aware that David wanted to speak to them on a very different subject.

All four of them made themselves comfortable and David started to tell of his first marriage. "Sylvia and I were loves young dream when we were first married, but as time went on Sylvia suffered so much. We both couldn't wait to have our own little family, and were devastated when our first baby was stillborn. We were told, don't worry it can't happen again but eighteen months later the dreadful experience repeated itself. We couldn't understand why it happened. No one could give us any advice, and looking back, I don't think very much support. Twice now she had gone into hospital to have a baby, and twice she had come home with nothing. At this stage, I wanted us to start looking into adoption, but very quickly Sylvia was pregnant again. This time she was different, she became so paranoid and anxious that at three months, she miscarried. And then the following year history repeated itself. It wasn't only physically, but mentally she was suffering too. When she felt well enough to travel, we decided on a holiday. A type of holiday we had never had before. So we set off on a four week cruise. By time we got home the old Sylvia was back. Whether it was the sun and sea air, or the good food and exciting new surroundings I don't know, but she started to be her old self. Then, to our surprise, she was pregnant and we both agreed that this would definitely be our last try. Making that decision seemed to help Sylvia, and it was like the four other babies had never happened.

We decided that this baby would be born in a private hospital, really just to break the pattern of before. Our baby was born and we were both ecstatically happy. You must understand that, the next 15 months were the happiest of Sylvia's life. She had all she had ever wanted, a husband, and baby. After the accident, it was Andrea that got me through it. My whole life had been ripped apart, and yet I had to pull myself together to look after our desperately ill baby. It frightens me even today to think that I could have lost them both.

Then one day, I was asked to design a conservatory. One of the new owners wanted to extend the cottage I had designed. By some kind of magic, I was standing in front of the most beautiful female I had ever seen, but not only that, she looked just like my daughter".

Caroline made a sudden little cough. "Excuse me, but can I get anyone a drink? Tea, coffee or a fruit drink?"

It was agreed by all that tea would be nice, and Caroline departed to the kitchen.

David watched Caroline leave the room and then turned to Evelyn and Veronica.

"Caroline still gets embarrassed when I pay her a compliment. It isn't something she grew up with".

Before David could continue, Evelyn spoke. "David, did you never ever consider that the baby you had seen on the day of her birth wasn't the same baby that you took home".

"Twice it crossed my mind, but they were fleeting moments. On the day Verity was born, I visited in the evening and Sylvia was sitting up in bed holding her wrapped in a thin shawl and her tiny little feet were poking out from underneath. Momentarily, I thought her feet looked a little blue, but the sun was bright and streaming through the window, and then when I glanced up at Sylvia she looked so incredibly happy that it just went out of my head. On the Sunday morning, I phoned the ward to see if there was anything I could take in for Sylvia. She said they were pleased I had called as Sylvia was in a bit of a state, and was it possible for me to go in straight away? I can tell you, my heart was beating so fast! We didn't have a phone, so I had called from a telephone box. I ran as fast as I could to my car and drove at I don't know what speed! On my arrival at the ward, the Sister called me into her office and explained that sadly a baby had passed away during the night and since Sylvia had heard, she was inconsolable. I could see that Sister hadn't exaggerated. Sylvia's face was one big red blotch from crying. With that, we heard a baby crying, it was Andrea. The nurse was wheeling her from the nursery for feeding. Andrea was passed to Sylvia and Sylvia was instantly calmed. Andrea was feeding from her so naturally, she only got distressed when Sylvia changed her on to her other breast. It was then that I noticed Andrea's feet. On the instep of her right foot there was a birthmark. I couldn't be certain, but I was sure it hadn't been there two days before. Again, the thought disappeared. It never crossed my mind again until after the car crash. By time I had arrived at Norwich hospital, the Doctors already knew that Andrea had a rare blood group and I knew it wasn't from me. When I played rugby as a teenager, I had a couple of serious injuries so I knew my blood group. When I told them that, they mumbled that it must have been Sylvia who had the rare blood group but I couldn't understand that. With all the treatment she had after losing the four babies why had no one mentioned it?

It was when Caroline told me she had donated blood, and I asked her when, did I really believe that Andrea wasn't my child. The child that I loved, the child that had given my wife 15 gloriously happy months. From the day I met Caroline and to the day I introduced Andrea to her, I assumed the babies had just got mixed up. Of course, the other problem was that I was forcing Caroline to own up to having been pregnant. I had truly fallen for Caroline. If I hadn't, I would never have become involved with her. For me, it was a relief that she could explain why there was this uncanny likeness. There were two things that Caroline had done for Verity: She convinced her parents that Verity could not have the name Sowersby-Smyth on her headstone, so she had 'Cooper', her real surname. I have to say, when I came along and her parents realised that was my name, Caroline had a difficult time to assure them that I was not her baby's Father. A very tricky moment, but quite true. At Verity's funeral, she laid flowers for Sylvia and me. Until the day of confessions she always placed flowers on Verity's grave on her correct birthday from Sylvia and myself. The day before Andrea's birthday. This just shows what a caring and loving person Caroline is".

Living With The Consequences

The room was quiet. David looked physically exhausted. It was then that Caroline came back with a tray laden with tea and cake.

Instinctively, she must have known what David was going to say. She sat next to him on the sofa and took his hand. Before anyone could say a word, a voice called from the hallway.

"Mum, Dad, where are you?"

Caroline looked up from her husband.

"It's Andrea, Andrea we are in the drawing room!"

The door was pushed open, and standing in the door way was a younger version of Caroline. Except, her hair was a light brown, and very curly, but she had the same big blue eyes and the stunning looks.

Caroline was up of the settee.

"Why are you home so early? Let me introduce you. Evelyn, Veronica, this is our daughter, Andrea. Andrea, this is Evelyn, who was a member of the staff at St.Agnes's, and her daughter Veronica. Evelyn was especially kind to me when you were born".

They both walked forward. Andrea started to speak.

"Hello, you would never believe it, but we went shopping first in Knightsbridge and guess who do you think we bumped into! Only Granny! She was with one of her friends, and they invited all five for us to Harrods for lunch and by time we came out and went to the theatre it was too late to get tickets, so we decided to come home. But walking back to the station, I saw this pair of shoes so we all had a great day".

By time she had finished, everyone was laughing.

It was left to David to explain to her that, during her whole recital of her day, she didn't take one breath.

By now it was 4pm, and Veronica thought that if they were still going to go see Verity's grave then perhaps they should be on their way.

Caroline had also realised that, for a lady in her seventies, it had been a long and emotional day for Evelyn but she dearly wanted her to see that she had kept her promise with Verity's grave. Caroline took control.

"I have just noticed the time, and I do so want to take you to Verity's grave. Evelyn, do you still feel up to it?"

"I most definitely do! " She looked at Veronica. "We do still have time and then I think we should make our way home".

Veronica agreed. Caroline suggested that, if Veronica followed her, then they could go home straight from the graveyard. Everyone was in agreement.

Evelyn gave David a peck on the cheek, and she gave Andrea a hug, which made Veronica feel quite emotional.

They made their way to the cars, and David and Andrea stood on the gravel drive to wave them goodbye.

Veronica and Evelyn didn't speak in the car. It was only when they got out that Evelyn realised she had bought nothing to place on the grave. She needn't have worried. Veronica went to her car boot and produced a beautiful posy of lemon and white flowers. Evelyn's favourite colours. Evelyn, overcome by her daughter's foresight, kissed her on the cheek.

"What would I have done without you? You must be the most special daughter anyone could ever ask for".

The three ladies walked along arm in arm with Evelyn holding the posy. They reached the spot under the oak tree where the tiny grave lay. Evelyn read out aloud the inscription:

> Verity Constance Cooper
> Whose short life touched
> Our Hearts forever
> 8th April 1960 to 9th April 1960

As Evelyn placed the posy on Verity's grave, all three women wiped a tear from their eye. Caroline backed away to leave the Mother and daughter some time on their own. The words on the gravestone were true. This tiny baby had been pivotal in so many lives.

Chapter Twenty Six

It had been a very long day. Evelyn and Veronica had hardly spoken in the car. They had been told so much, some of it extremely sad, and then out of that sadness, extreme happiness. Who would believe that a Mother gives her baby up, and then by pure chance, becomes her Mother again! Only thirty minutes away from home and Veronica realised that her Mother was asleep. She gently called her name, and Evelyn awoke with a start.

"Mum, would you like to come and stay with Edward and I tonight? We can go past the Willows and collect some clean clothes for tomorrow. Then tomorrow, you and I can talk over all we were told today".

"Veronica, that would be lovely but I have taken so much of your time already. Haven't you anything planned for tomorrow?"

"We had, but Edward can go on his own. The boys have a cricket match at school. As they are both in the team I won't be seeing much of them, and you know I do find it a little boring. It's just if you go back to the Willows tonight I am going to worry about you".

It was agreed that Evelyn would stay the one night, and Veronica drove on to the Willows so that they could let the staff know Evelyn would be away for the night and to pack a small bag. While they were there Veronica phoned home and asked if Edward could start supper for the three of them.

By time they had eaten, Evelyn looked totally exhausted. Veronica went and put a hot water bottle in the bed in the guest room. She didn't think the bed needed airing, but she did think it would make it feel cosy.

After a cup of tea in the lounge, Veronica took her Mother upstairs. They said goodnight to each other and Veronica told her Mother not to worry what time she got up in the morning it was going to be a lazy day for both of them. When Veronica returned down stairs, Edward offered her a whisky, which Veronica accepted.

"I didn't like to ask in front of your Mother, but you both came in smiling so I assumed it was a successful day?"

"Successful isn't really the right word, it has such an amazing ending, but you do know I still can't tell you. It really is my Mother's business, but I think after today she may tell you".

"Look Veronica, I have said all along I don't need to know, I am just concerned that you are both ok".

"We are, that's why I wanted Mum to stay so we can talk about it tomorrow. Neither of us spoke about it in the car. There was just too much to think about".

Chapter Twenty Seven

Edward managed to get up out of bed without disturbing Veronica, who was sound asleep. He picked up his golfing clothes, car keys and wallet, and quietly made his way to his son's bathroom the far end of the landing. Here he showered and dressed. After loading his golf clubs into his car, he set off for his golf club and breakfast in the clubhouse.

Back at The Chimneys, Veronica and Evelyn both slept on. At 9.20am, the phone rang. It immediately woke Veronica up and before she knew what she was doing she had grabbed the receiver which was on her bedside cabinet.

"Hello, who is it?"

The gruff voice of a fourteen year old male answered.

 "Hello Mum, twin 2 here".

 Veronica's sons had never referred to themselves by name when speaking to their Mother, they always thought it more fun to refer to their birth order.

"Hello Paul, You gave me a fright! I was still asleep, what on earth is the time?"

"It's nearly 9.30am, what were you doing last night, you are alright? You aren't ill?"

Veronica was now fully awake.

"That is very nice of you to ask but I was out with Nanna yesterday, and we had quite a long day. Actually Paul, I must go and see if she is alright, stay there".

Veronica grabbed her dressing gown and made her way to the guest room. Gently tapping on the door she waited for an answer.

"Come in. Oh Veronica have you seen the time? I think we have overslept!"

Veronica, so pleased to see her Mother sitting up and looking refreshed,

"It was the phone that woke me. It's Paul, now I know you are ok I'll go and see what he wants".

"Paul, sorry I'm back now, what was it".

Veronica could hear laughter now, and her twin 1 had joined his brother.

"Mum, what's this? You and Nanna were out for the day yesterday and now sleeping it off!"

"I suppose neither of you will let me forget this morning, so what can I do for you? And while I remember, Dad will be on his own this afternoon. Nanna and I have unfinished business".

She was now smiling 'that will give them something to wonder about' she thought.

Paul now had the phone again. "Mum, we were wondering if Dad could bring our new cricket bats with him, the ones we had for our birthdays, and some more pocket money would be great".

"I will see what I can do, I hope it goes well for you both this afternoon. See you in a couple of weeks. Take care".

The boys called out together. "Thank you, bye Mum, bye".

The phone line went dead. They had rung off. Veronica put the receiver down and started to think about her and her Mother's breakfast.

By 11 o'clock, Veronica and Evelyn were both dressed and back down stairs in the kitchen. "Mum, do you mind if we don't have a traditional roast today? I thought if I cooked the chicken we could have it with new potatoes and salad. Not such a heavy meal for Edward to eat before he sets of for the boy's school".

"That suits me fine dear, then perhaps this afternoon we could talk about yesterday. I did wonder if we could ask them back here, because when I have gone over everything in my head at times, I thought Caroline was unsure how my life planned out. Then I could show her the Willows and how successful mine and your Father's joint venture was".

"Mum that sounds a lovely idea. We will sort some dates out and if you like I can ring her this week".

After, the light lunch had been eaten, Edward left for his afternoon of cricket. Taking with him, two new cricket bats and cash in his wallet.

Veronica and Evelyn cleared away the dirty dishes, and with the kettle onto boil, Evelyn made herself comfortable in the lounge. Veronica followed shortly with a tray of tea things but neither of them made any effort to pour out the tea. Instead they immediately started to talk about the previous day's revelations.

"Mum, I think yesterday could not have gone any better. I still find it hard to believe the coincidence of Caroline meeting David, him being free, and for them both to fall in love with each other. What I really liked, and I know Caroline had promised that Verity would be buried properly, but to have David's name on the headstone and lay flowers on his and Sylvia's behalf, I think it just proves what a nice girl Caroline is".

Evelyn couldn't agree more, but what she next had to say to Veronica did surprise her.

"This afternoon I would like to go back to the Willows. I can't stress enough how all my worries have been laid to rest, and that is all due to you. This morning, I have been thinking about things, and I know my will is held with John Featherstone but I have a couple of items that I really want to leave to certain people, to do this do I have to go and see him?"

"Mum, can I ask what they are or is it very personal? No, don't answer that. I will make arrangements for you to see John, but in the meantime if it helps, you could right their names on a piece of paper and slip it into the items. Does that help?"

"That sounds perfect, thank you. Now if it is alright with you I am going to pack my bits and pieces, and I will be ready when you are".

Evelyn was back at the Willows just after 4 O'clock. Veronica carried her overnight bag in for her. When they reached Evelyn's room, she followed her Mother in and started to unpack the few bits inside.

"Veronica, don't worry about that now. Come and sit over here I would like to talk to you". Veronica did as she was asked and sat in the opposite armchair, both chairs facing out in to the well kept garden of the Willows.

Taking Veronica's hand, Evelyn started to speak. "I am not sure if you have known how much I missed your Father when he died. I don't mean the first couple of years, I mean more recently. I have been a widow now for 13 years, and instead of getting used to it and missing him less, I seem to miss him more".

Veronica could feel herself getting emotional, it was something she had never given any thought to. Her Father died shortly before her Mother was due to retire and instead she carried on working at the home until retiring in 1969 at the age of 63.

"Mum, I am so sorry, I should have realised. What can I do, there must be something?" Evelyn smiled back at her daughter.

"Veronica, I am not telling you so that you can do something for me. I want you to know because, in some ways the only thing that has kept me going is hoping one day I would be able to find out about Caroline. That doesn't mean I don't love you or Michael or your families, but your Father always made me feel that we were part of each other. Now I am going to apologise, I don't think I am making myself very clear".

"Mum, I do understand. In some ways, as a child, no, teenager, I used to feel that I was on the outside looking in where you and Dad were concerned. It didn't upset me because I was rather proud that you both felt that way about each other. I certainly had a number of friends whose parents I don't think even liked each other, let alone loved each other".

" I am so pleased we have had this little chat because saying thank you for sorting out my mess doesn't seem a big enough reward. I feel a huge weight has been lifted off my shoulders. A weight I have been carrying around for years. Now I can fully relax and reminisce".

Veronica, who had been looking out at the garden so she could keep herself composed, quickly turned her head.

"Mum you are feeling ok, you aren't unwell are you?"

Patting Veronica's hand Evelyn answered.
"I am feeling the best I have felt in many years,
don't worry. As I said, yesterday has made me
feel that my life is now in order. Now off you go
and make that lovely husband of yours a nice
supper for when he gets back from the twin's
school".
Both ladies got up out of their chairs and made
their way back through the reception area to
the main entrance.
Veronica spoke,
"I will pop by during the week, Good bye Mum".
"Goodbye my Darling, and thank you".
Veronica walked to her car, waved back to her
Mother. She started the engine, reversed out of
the parking space and with another wave, drove
off.
While she was waiting at the one set of traffic
lights on her journey home, she realised that
they hadn't made a date for inviting Caroline
and her family over to the Willows.
To herself she thought,' I must remind Mum
when I next see her'.

Chapter Twenty Eight

Monday morning, Veronica was back in the office. She had a number of appointments but she desperately wanted to make enough time to phone Harold Brownlow.

It wasn't until much later when Veronica found she had a window of at least 45minutes. She spoke to her secretary and told her that she mustn't be disturbed for the next hour and then dialled Harold's number.

The receiver was picked up straight away and Veronica could hear the clear voice of the retired Chief Inspector,

"Hello Harold, it's Veronica Cousins".

"Good afternoon Mrs Cousins, and how are you and Mrs Compton?"

"Yes, we are both well thank you for asking, actually my Mother is more than in good health. Our visit on Saturday to Caroline Cooper's was a complete success! It could not have gone any better. You were quite right about the grave my Mother wanted located. Caroline offered the information and took us herself. I feel that my Mother and I are indebted to you for finding Caroline and for the initial introduction back into her life".

"Well that is very kind of you to say so. A very nice young lady, I thought. I had my doubts when you asked me to take the job on, as you can never take it for granted how someone will respond, but I thought her to be a very genuine person".

"My Mother found it very reassuring that all was well with herself and family. We haven't discussed fees, the same arrangement as before. You submit your invoice to me personally and I will post you a cheque".

"Well Mrs Cousins that is very good of you but I don't want payment. Had you not recommended me to your Mother, then I wouldn't have known that Judge Sowersby-Smith had passed away. He was a good person, and professionally we went back a long way. One of the old school, and it enabled me to pay my respects. It's nice to be able to do something for a fellow human being and telling me that all went well on Saturday is enough payment, but thank you for asking".

"Harold, I don't know what to say. That is so kind of you. Look, if at anytime I can be of help to you or your wife, then please do not hesitate to contact me so that I can return your kindness".

"I will bear that in mind, thank you. Just one thing, have you any plans to see Caroline again?"

"Yes, we do. Caroline wants to see the Willows, where my Mother now lives, but also because that was the business that my parents started after the incident with Caroline. I suppose my Mother wanted to go and see how Caroline's life has turned out on her home territory, now Caroline wants to do the same. I am looking forward to their visit, we just need to get something in the diary ".
Harold replied, "I am very pleased to hear it".
After pleasantries were exchanged, Veronica replaced the receiver.

Harold was feeling quite chuffed with himself. He found as his career had progressed, the feeling of a good days work diminished. The criminals were more hardened, and the crime more brutal. This little investigation only took one phone call and some ingenuity and experience. He must remember to tell Edna when she gets home that Veronica Cousins was extremely pleased with him, and that anytime they need the services of a Solicitor to let her know.

Chapter Twenty Nine

The following morning, Veronica and Edward were in the kitchen having just finished their breakfast when the phone rang. Edward got up to answer it.

"Hello".

"Hello, it is Yvonne Kelly here, is Veronica there?"

"Yes she is Yvonne, hold on she is coming to the phone".

Veronica got up from her chair and was mouthing to Edward that Yvonne Kelly was likely to keep her talking for ages and she had a busy day ahead of her. To her surprise Edward held out the phone and grabbed his chair so that Veronica could sit down.

"Hello, Yvonne how can I help?"

"Veronica, I am very sorry to have to tell you, but your Mother passed away during the night. I have already called her GP he is on his way. The carer went into wake her as she hadn't come down for breakfast. I have been to see her, she looks very peaceful laying in bed. Please accept my condolences".

Veronica sat motionless on the chair. When she heard Yvonne's voice stop she spoke.

"Can I come to the Willows now?"

"Yes, I thought you would want to, please come as soon as you are ready to. We won't move her. I am so sorry Veronica".

Veronica could hear another voice in the back ground.

"Veronica I am sorry, I must go the Doctor has just arrived".

"Yes, thank you for letting me know, goodbye". Edward stepped forward and took the phone out of his wife's hand. She had gone very white. "Edward, I can't believe she has just gone! Can you phone Ian for me, he will probably still be at home. I need to check my diary. Actually, Margaret can take care of that, I must phone Michael. What time will it be in Sydney?" Edward looked at his watch.

"Well they are ten hours ahead, so about 6pm. I will ring Ian for you now from the study phone. It will be better that he knows before he gets to the office. Then you can sit there and ring Michael, and then we will leave for the Willows".

Veronica nodded in agreement. The study was really Edward's second office, and as such had its own phone and phone number.

Veronica picked up the address book by the telephone and looked for her brother's phone number. It wasn't a number she had ever been able to remember, far too many digits.

Veronica dialled his number and then waited impatiently for it to ring at the other end.
Then after what seemed like ages, the phone was being picked up and it was a child's voice Veronica heard.
"Hello, who is it?"
It was Veronica's 9 year old niece. She didn't feel in the mood for small talk.
"Hello Amanda, is Daddy there or if not Mummy? It is Auntie Veronica".
"Daddy is home, he is just having a swim in the pool. I will tell him you are on the phone, bye".
"Thank you Amanda, good bye".
Veronica was finding it hard now to control her emotions, and as soon as she heard the phone being picked up and Michael's voice she burst into tears.
"Veronica what has happened, is it Mum?"
All Michael could hear was his sister's tears. He knew that it was something extremely important, and patiently waited for her to collect herself.
"I am so sorry Michael I just couldn't control myself. It's Mum, she passed away during the night. Yvonne Kelly has just phoned. Mum was found this morning still in bed as though she was just asleep. I am going with Edward now to the Home. What should I do? I just can't think straight".
Everyone who knew Michael thought that his vocation as a Doctor was well chosen. He had

the perfect bedside manner, and this he used with his sister.

"Veronica, you have had a terrible shock. It's not something anyone would think was imminently going to happen. I am pleased Edward is with you, and perhaps when you have maybe seen Mum, then ring me. I meanwhile will go through my workload, and Jenny can start phoning airlines so that we can get a flight back. Is that all ok?"

"Yes that's a plan, and hopefully Mum's GP will still be at the home so he might be able to tell us what happens next. Don't book any tickets until I ring you back. Oh Michael, it's so sad, speak soon".

"Goodbye Sis, yes speak soon".

With that Veronica ended the call, and while she was waiting for Edward to join her in the kitchen, she started to stack the dirty dishes already for Mrs Davis. As Edward joined Veronica, she was busy writing a note for Mrs Davis letting her know where they were going and why. Now she was already planning ahead, and was asking Mrs Davis for a list of jobs she thought would be needed to be done for the wake to be held at the Chimneys.

When Veronica and Edward arrived at the home, they signed themselves in and turned to

see her Mother's GP coming out of Yvonne
Kelly's office.

Dr Hall knew Veronica and Edward quite well
due to their association with the home. He
extended his hand to shake theirs and gave a
slight nod of the head to indicate his
condolences before he spoke.

"Mr and Mrs Cousins, please accept my
condolences but I am afraid I can't stop, I have
another urgent call to attend to. But I have
spoken to Miss Kelly who will tell you of the
next formalities, and please ring me anytime on
the surgery number and I will endeavour to
answer any questions you may have, goodbye".

They both thanked him, and Dr Hall was out of
the main entrance and running to his car.

When they both turned back, Yvonne Kelly was
holding her office door open and beckoning
them in.

"Veronica, Edward please accept my
condolences. Dr Hall has confirmed your
Mother's passing but he is unable to write a
death certificate because your Mother had not
been seen by a Doctor in the last three weeks. It
looks like a post-mortem, I am sorry. Look, we
can talk all about that later. Would you like to
see your Mother now?"

Veronica was already standing up from her
chair, she replied.

"Yes please".

With that the three of them made their way to Evelyn's room. The bedroom curtains had been drawn out of respect, and a large floral display that normally stood in the reception area had been placed on the coffee table. Another respectful gesture.

Yvonne discreetly with drew from the room and gently closed the door.

Veronica breathed a sigh of relief, she was dreading there being an audience when she was undoubtedly going to break down.

She wasn't sure what she expected to see, but unexpectedly, Evelyn did look very peaceful, and as though she was in a deep sleep. The tears rolled down Veronica's cheeks, and Edward held her hand, deeply upset himself. He had always had a lovely relationship with both of his wife's parents. Neither of them could say how long they stood looking down at Evelyn. Eventually Veronica's tears stopped, and she took another clean tissue from her handbag and dabbed her eyes.

They made their way to the door, and turned and looked one final time, then slowly made their way back to Yvonne's office.

After coffee was ordered for all three of them. Yvonne felt guilty, but broached the subject of ownership of the Willows.

"I know it isn't the right time to ask, but some of the residents, and certainly some of their families, are going to want to know if the home will have to close".

Yvonne looked distinctly embarrassed, but knew she also had members of staff who, although would be sad at the passing of Evelyn, would also be concerned about the security of their jobs.

Veronica and Edward, both of them being professional people, understood the significance of this question and probably, placed in similar circumstances to Yvonne, would have asked the same. But Veronica forgetting this was terse with her answer.

"Yvonne, my Mother isn't cold yet!" and promptly bursted into tears again.

Edward continued for her,

"It has always been agreed that in the event of this happening the home would not close. Veronica is a joint owner with her Mother, and because neither Evelyn or Veronica are active in the running of the home, it was also agreed that Michael would join the board in Evelyn's place. Veronica did exactly this after the death of her Father. Please let all interested parties know that nothing is set to change. I hope that is helpful".

"Yes, thank you, most helpful. As you can appreciate, a lot of the staff have a mortgage to pay. Now, Dr Hall has indicated that by the end of today we should know what is going to happen. Obviously your Mother's door will remain locked, but if you want to take any valuables today then please do so. But at no time will anybody be allowed in her room unaccompanied by a senior member of staff". Veronica looked shocked that anyone would contemplate taking any belongings while her Mother was still in her room.

The coffee arrived and more general things were discussed: which funeral company, the Service, and venue for the wake. Yvonne offered the use of the Willows which seemed a bit odd, as Veronica being a co-owner she wouldn't need to be asked, but it was merely a formality. After they had finished their coffee, Veronica and Edward rose to go. Yvonne went with them out to their car. She shook hands with Edward, but kissed Veronica on the cheek. For the first time that day, Veronica and Edward saw her drop her reserve and the private persona of Yvonne Kelly showed through, and so did her grief.

On their return home, Veronica went to the phone in Edward's study, and sat in his chair and proceeded to telephone her brother. This time it was a much longer call. Brother and sister at different times, both broke down and were comforted by the other. It was agreed that Michael would start to delegate his work load. To do this comfortably he and his family would not fly home for another two weeks. This would mean that all the organising for the funeral and wake would fall to Veronica. Fortunately for Veronica, Edward had spoken to both of her partners that morning and they had insisted that she concentrate on family matters, so Veronica could reassure Michael that she could indeed take on this task.

After refreshment, Edward phoned their sons school and spoke to the Headmaster. It was agreed that Veronica and Edward should visit the boys that afternoon. The Headmaster suggested that both boys, being close to their Grandmother, may prefer to be taken out of school and perhaps return later in the evening. It was a good suggestion, and after the initial upset by the twins, all four of them left the school and Edward drove them to Milton, a small town near the school, where they walked through the park. Later, they chose an Italian restaurant to have some dinner before returning the twins back to school. Edward went to thank the Headmaster for his understanding, and to let him know that the boys wanted to attend their Grandmother's funeral and that, Veronica or he, would be in contact as soon as the arrangements were made. By time Edward had returned to the car, Veronica had fallen asleep. He hoped he could start the car without disturbing her but she instantly sat up, and appeared to be wide awake.

"Edward, it has been such a long day and I still haven't phoned any relations yet. I do feel better about Andrew and Paul. When we told them they were so upset, at least we have been able to spend some time with them. And they did grasp the fact that it was all so peaceful".

"Darling don't start worrying about the boys. They have got each other, Mr Burrows has said that the staff will keep an eye on them, and if there is a problem he will immediately be in touch. You have agreed to take on a lot now. When you say relations, who were you thinking of?"

"Well, we aren't a big family so really it is only Auntie Marie and her daughter, Patricia. Mum didn't have any cousins, being an only child whose parents were only children. I am worried it will be a bit late to phone Aunt Marie, as Dad's older sister, she is a number of years older than Mum. What do you think?"

The roads home had been quite empty, and Edward was now turning into their drive. He stopped the car and faced his wife.

"Let's go in and have a drink, I wouldn't phone Aunt Marie. Phone Patricia, tell her and ask when would it be the best time to phone. Then after you have done that we will have our drink and an early night".

Veronica readily agreed, she was starting to feel completely fatigued.

When she rang, Patricia immediately offered her condolences, but suggested that, as her Mother was well into her eighties, would Veronica mind if she told her Mother herself, and did it the following morning? Then, she could spend the rest of the day with her. Now days, her Mother took hearing the news of friends and family passing away quite badly, and with the loss of her Sister in law, it would bring back the memories of the loss of her younger brother. Veronica thought that would be a kind way to deliver the news to her elderly Aunt. She realised that Aunt Marie was not going to be the only difficult phone call to make. They said goodnight to each other, and Veronica felt she was dragging her body back to the lounge where Edward was waiting for her with, she hoped a large whisky and soda.

The next day, Veronica had planned to start early to make the sad phone calls, of informing friends, relatives, financial institutions and Government bodies. She had made herself comfortable in Edward's study, and closed the door. The last thing she wanted was to be interrupted by Mrs Davis or the household appliances. She was so focused on her list of calls that when the phone rang, it made her jump. She grabbed the receiver!
"Hello".

"Hello, Mrs Cousins?"

"Yes, speaking".

"Hello, this is Mr Walters from the Coroners office regarding the late Mrs Compton. It is in regard of a post-mortem".

Veronica was very quiet, so Mr Walters continued,

"Due to the fact that your Mother had not seen a Doctor in the last three weeks, it will be necessary for there to be a post-mortem to ascertain the cause of death. This is to be arranged for this afternoon, and this morning her body will be collected from the Willows .As soon as the results are known then, myself or my colleague will be touch. Have you been in touch with the funeral directors yet?"

"No, not yet I haven't. I thought it better to wait until we knew exactly what was happening. Is it ok now for me to do that?"

"Yes by all means. In fact, when we contact you next, if you have the name and address of the company then it would be very helpful. If there is nothing else, please accept my condolences and we will be in touch as soon as we can, goodbye Mrs Cousins".

"Goodbye Mr Walters, and thank you".

She replaced the receiver and sat there stunned. Who would believe in such a short time, everything concerning her Mother had completely changed. She knew that if she didn't carry on and make the next call, then she would break down again and as strange as it sounded she was far too busy. Abandoning the next call on her list, she phoned Yvonne Kelly.

Yvonne picked up straight away and wasn't surprised to hear Veronica's voice, after all it had only been 10 minutes ago that the Coroners office had called. They had informed Yvonne of the post-mortem and collection of the body, and had let her know that they would contact Mrs Cousins.

After the niceties, Veronica explained about the Coroner's call. Yvonne thought at these times the less said the better and let Veronica think she was passing on new information. It was agreed by both ladies that Veronica would go to the Willows the following day, not to clear her Mother's room, but to remove any valuables, documents and personnel effects.

She spent all morning on the phone, and at 12pm she heard a car pull up on the drive. She looked out the window and to her delight it was Edward. She rushed to the front door to let him in, and threw her arms around him. He was a little startled, but realised the great emotional stress his wife was under.

While Veronica prepared cheese on toast for them, she recapped the phone call from the Coroners office. Edward wasn't at all surprised with the outcome and suggested that perhaps she could contact the funeral Directors that they had used for his parents. They were not the nearest, but they had been reliable and had a lot of dignity. Veronica was so grateful at Edward's suggestion, another awful task dealt with.

After Edward had left to go back to the office, Veronica carried on making phone calls. Firstly to Wakelings, the Funeral Directors, their professionalism made the call for Veronica much easier than she had anticipated. She made an appointment for the Saturday, when all the arrangements would be made, and this included the venue for the wake. Veronica had planned for it to be at the Chimneys. It was suggested by Mr Wakeling that as her Mother had friends residing at the Willows and it was her and her husbands dream, would it be better held there? She understood the reasoning, and would seriously give it some thought.

It was back to personnel calls now. Some were obviously harder than others, and most of her Mother's friends wanted to reminisce with happy memories they shared with Evelyn.

At 4 o'clock, Veronica decided to stretch her legs and make herself a refreshing cup of tea. She had just poured herself out a cup, when the phone rang.

"Good afternoon, is that Mrs Cousins?"

Veronica didn't recognise the voice.

"Yes it is, can I ask who is calling?"

"I am Mr Hains, from the Coroner's office. I understand you spoke to my colleague Mr Walters this morning".

"Yes I did, have you the results already?"

"We do have the preliminary results, but this will enable you to make the arrangements with your Funeral Director. Now I can tell you the Pathologist report over the phone or would you rather wait and receive it in the post? It isn't complete, as there are two results waiting to come back, but the Pathologist has stated that they are a formality and will have no significant bearing on his findings".

"I think Mr Hains, I would rather you told me now".

"The cause of death was a massive stroke. The Pathologist has commented that it would have been very quick, and as such your Mother would have been totally unaware. He would also like you to know that there wouldn't have been anything anyone could have done for her had she not been on her own. He has made a point of that, and wished you to know. Obviously, the report has a lot more detail, and once complete it will be posted to you. Have you been in contact with an undertaker?"

"Yes, I have we are going to use Wakelings".

"I will fill that in on our paperwork, and I will contact them and make arrangements with them directly regarding the collection of your

Mother. Please accept my condolences, goodbye".

Veronica replaced the receiver. He managed to answer the question which had been bothering Veronica since the very first call from the Willows Manager, nothing could have been done to save her Mother.

Now she knew the cause of death, she couldn't put off any longer the phone call she was dreading. She picked up the receiver once again, and dialled the number, hoping that no one would pick up.

Chapter Thirty

"Hello Caroline". Veronica's voice was very somber but Caroline hadn't noticed, she was genuinely excited to hear Veronica's voice.
"Hello Veronica, I have been looking forward to you calling. Have you and Evelyn got some dates for when we can get together again?"
Veronica didn't know what to say, and just sat holding the receiver. Caroline's voice trailed away.
"Veronica, are you still there? What has happened? Something has happened what is it?"
"Caroline, Mum passed away in the early hours of Tuesday morning".
"Oh no!" Then all Veronica could hear down the telephone was Caroline crying.
It seemed like an eternity before Caroline was able to control her emotions. When she did, Veronica spoke.
"I have just spoken to the Coroner's office, and Mum had a massive stroke. There was nothing anyone could have done and it happened while she was asleep so she wouldn't have known anything about it. I have been worrying that perhaps last weekend was too much for her but

thinking now, she was very happy when I took her back to the Willows on Sunday. She had done what she wanted to do before it was too late, and that was to meet up with you".

"Veronica, I am so sorry. I am at a true loss of knowing what to say to you. Look, if there is anything I can do for you, please don't hesitate to ask. Have you any arrangements made yet?"

"On Saturday Edward and I will be seeing the Undertaker, and if it is alright, can I ring you and let you know?"

"Of course, David and I will both be there. But, how are you? Is your brother able to help?"

"No, at the moment he is still in Australia. As a Paediatrician, it is very difficult for him just to drop everything although of course he would have done if Mum had been ill. Once we know the date for the funeral, then he will book their flights. They won't have any trouble in getting flights.

Caroline, I am so pleased you will be there, not only for Mum but for me as well".

She couldn't say anymore, she knew that it wouldn't take much more for her to lose control.

They said goodbye, knowing that they would be speaking again quite soon.

The next two days flew by. With all Veronica's phone calls made until she had the arrangements for the funeral, she decided to go to the Willows and speak with Yvonne regarding the wake. She also knew that she needed to visit her Mother's room and remove any valuables and documents.

First things first, after parking her car, she made her way to Yvonne's office. She didn't want to make it a long meeting. Going to the home knowing Evelyn would never be there again felt so raw, after all it was still only a number of days.

Yvonne was unusually quiet, and this made it easier for Veronica to concentrate on the pros and cons of having the wake at the Willows. It was jointly decided that, due to some residents not feeling up to going to the funeral but still wanted to pay their respects, the wake would take place at the Willows but the funeral would leave from the Chimneys. It made sense, after all the Willows had been her parent's business enterprise, of which they were both inordinately proud off. This was a way of publicly acknowledging it.

After her meeting with Yvonne, Veronica went to her Mother's room. She unlocked the door and quietly went in. The curtains were open and the sun was shining in. She made her way to the french windows, and opened them wide. Then she put her handbag down on the bed. She walked towards the dressing table, as she did there was a knock at the door which startled her.

"Come in".

It was Linda, one of the day staff.

"Hello Mrs Cousins, I saw you come in and I didn't want to disturb you. I know what it is like, I have been there, but I just wondered if I could get you a coffee or pot of tea?"

"Linda that's very kind, a cup of coffee would be lovely. Can I ask you a favour? Only yourself and Yvonne know I am here, and at the moment I don't feel up to the residents coming and passing on their condolences. I know it sounds ungrateful, but I just want to remove Mum's personal papers and be gone".

"As I said Mrs Cousins, I do know how it feels. I have lost both my parents as well so don't worry I won't let on that I have seen you. Although a word of advice, if you want to leave unnoticed wait until 12.40pm when everyone is having lunch. Even the stragglers will be down by then".

She turned and gently opened the door, peeped out, and then was gone.

Within minutes, she was back carrying a tray with a coffee pot, cup and saucer, milk jug and a plate of chocolate digestives. Veronica looked at the tray.

"How do you know about the biscuits".

Linda smiled." Your Mother often told me that when she had a difficult task ahead, a chocolate biscuit worked wonders". She gave Veronica a wink and was gone.

Veronica opened the top drawer of her
Mother's dressing table, and started the
onerous job of going through her Mother's
possessions.

When her parents opened the home, they
wanted each resident to feel safe with all of
their belongings, especially jewellery and
personnel documents. They decided the best
way would be to have a carpenter fit an inner
door with a proper lock on one of the
compartments in the wardrobe.

Once Veronica had checked the dressing table
and found only clothing, she knew that it would
be necessary to look in her Mother's handbag
for the key. Once she located the key, she made
her way to the wardrobe. On opening it, she
thought about what a clever idea the safe was.
It was quite a size, as it went as far back as the
wardrobe. Inside, Veronica could see many
jewellery boxes, and some paperwork. She
emptied it out onto the dressing table top. To
her surprise, there were two jewellery boxes,
one large, and one ring box that had been
labelled. Next to these, sitting in the safe were
three envelopes. Two of the envelopes had the
same names on as the boxes and the third was
addressed to Veronica.

She took her envelope, and sat in one of the
armchairs facing the window. She poured
herself out a cup of coffee. She then slit the

envelope open, removed the note inside and very wearily started to read;

Date 19th June 1978

My dearest Veronica,
I have bequeathed you all of my jewellery and my personal belongings but there are two special requests I want to make. And so, my darling daughter, will you kindly pass on the letters and boxes to those named.
I know that I can rely on you totally as I have done when I so needed help.
With all my love and thanks
Mumx

Veronica placed the letter down on the tray, and searched for her hankie as the tears were once again streaming down her face.

As advised by Linda, Veronica signed herself out at 12.45pm. She had done what she had set out to do and packed in her Mother's overnight hold-all was all of her Mother's valuables.

On the Saturday morning, Veronica and Edward went to Wakelings the undertakers. Mr Wakeling remembered them both on sight. All of the arrangements were made for ten days time. This would give Michael and his family plenty of time to readjust from their long journey from Australia . Evelyn's wishes had been quite straightforward, as she was to be buried with her husband in a double plot. The wake was now going to be at the Willows, so far less work for Veronica and her daily help, Mrs Davis.

Michael and family flew in to Heathrow airport on the Friday morning. They collected their luggage got a taxi, and arrived at Veronica's looking extremely tired. Veronica was waiting at the front door as soon as she saw the taxi drive up. Once her two nieces were out of the car, they ran towards their Aunt for a welcome hug. Lindsey, who looked very much like Jennifer, her Mother, was now 11 and Amanda, who was 9, favoured her Grandmother Evelyn.

The time from Michael's arrival to Tuesday the day of Evelyn's funeral passed very quickly. By the Saturday evening, Veronica and Edward had a full house, the twins Andrew and Paul were now home from school for their Grandmother's funeral, and enjoying seeing their little cousins. For Veronica, it was a time that she and her brother reminisced about their parents and child hood. Michael and Jennifer also took the time to say their goodbyes to Evelyn, in the Chapel of Rest. Flowers were chosen, a menu confirmed for the wake, and appropriate clothes bought.

Evelyn's funeral, like all funerals was very sad.
The only comfort that Veronica and Michael
could take was the amount of friends, family
and old colleagues that attended and paid their
last respects. As Veronica stood to leave the
church, she glanced over the congregation.
There were people who she had never even
contacted, but by word of mouth had found out
and were there. It was a very comforting
feeling.
After the interment, the funeral cars left for the
Willows followed by a long procession of
private cars.
Yvonne had well and truly worked very hard
with all her staff, and somehow had managed
to cater for the unknown amount of guests.
Within a couple of hours, people started to
leave and say their goodbyes. The residents
who had attended, left, and only a small group
of mourners were left. Amongst these were
Caroline, David and Andrea.
Caroline had been introduced to everyone as a
former patient in Evelyn's midwifery days.
Veronica approached Caroline, who was in
conversation with Yvonne. As Veronica
approached, Caroline spoke.
"Veronica, Yvonne has just been telling me the
amazing job your parents did when taking the
Willows on. It must have been some task,
turning a run down Manor House into a
residential home!"

"It was indeed, but because they knew what they wanted to achieve when they viewed this property, they instantly knew it had potential". With that Yvonne interrupted.

"Would you mind if I pop back to my office, I am trying to get hold of one of the resident's Dentist, and the practice suggested I phoned back at this time. I shouldn't be too long".

With that she disappeared. Veronica was feeling relieved, she really wanted to speak to Caroline alone.

"Caroline, I was so hoping to see you on your own today. Would you mind if we went and had a walk in the garden?"

Caroline was a little mystified, but readily agreed. Once they had moved away from the house, Veronica explained.

"As you probably know, I have had to start looking through my Mother's things. It's funny, I always knew that my Father loved to buy Mum jewellery, but I never realised until I took it home how much there was. While I was looking for it, oh look, there is an empty bench let's sit down. As I was saying, I don't feel I am making a very good job of this".

With that, Veronica opened her handbag and took out an envelope and a ring box. She handed them both to Caroline.

"What I am trying to say is, these are for you, I don't know what it is or what Mum has written, but she did leave me a letter asking me to pass them on".

Caroline was looking quite shocked, after all Evelyn had only come back into her life a matter of weeks ago.

"Veronica I am not sure that she should be giving me anything".

"Look, if it makes you feel any better why don't you wait until you have opened it".

"Yes, that makes sense, in fact I'll open it now". Gently, Caroline removed the sellotape. Then she opened the lid to see the most beautiful Art Deco Sapphire ring she had ever seen. She gasped.

"Veronica I can't accept this! It is beautiful, but it should be yours. Do you think she was well when she did this?"

Veronica was smiling at her new friend.

"I think she was quite well, don't open the letter now. Read that at home but I am sure there is an explanation and as to you having it. I have always believed that just because you are family it doesn't mean you should automatically inherit what ever it may be. Please wear it and enjoy it, because I am sure that is what Mum would have wanted".

Caroline slipped the envelope and ring box into her handbag. She wasn't convinced that it was appropriate, but she decided to wait until she read Evelyn's letter.

Arm in arm they walked back to the Manor House, now the Willows, where conversation turned to Michael.

"Veronica, how long is Michael and Jennifer staying?"

"They are going to stay until Saturday. When Mum retired after Dad passed away, and she moved into the home, all her finances were sorted. Other than her personal effects, there isn't very much to be done. It's all very straightforward for her Solicitor. Michael and I have managed to spend quite a lot of time together, and we think it's about time we went out to Australia and see his home and way of life. So we are planning to be there for Christmas and New Year, which will be nice for all of us to be together, especially as it will be the first Christmas that Mum won't be here".

"That sounds a lovely idea. Why don't you and Edward come and stay with us the weekend after. The men can have a game of golf, and I would appreciate your opinion of my choice of soft furnishings for the bedrooms and conference suite. I think your house is so tastefully decorated. You have a real flair!"

Veronica looked at Caroline.

"You do know, that could have been Edward's input?"

They looked at each other and burst out laughing.

The Solicitors was really a formality for Veronica and Michael. They had known the contents of their Mother's will for many years. Michael was to become a non working Director on the board of Directors taking his Mother's place.

Very soon it was Saturday, time for them to say goodbye. Andrew and Paul had gone back to school on the Thursday, and their little cousins were sad to see them go.

Once Veronica and Edward could no longer see the taxi that was taking them back to Heathrow airport, Veronica closed the front door with a sigh.

"That's that, back to work on Monday. I think I am looking forward to having a routine again. What do you think?"

"I think I am glad to have my wife back again. Veronica, we are both going to miss your Mum very much, but yes, it will be good to get back to what we know, and next weekend we are going to Caroline and David's. It is a funny thing but I do feel as though we have known them for ages".

"So do I, but I still have one more little job to do first".

Chapter Thirty One

Monday morning, Veronica was back in the office for 8 o'clock. She had phoned Margaret, her secretary, on Friday and true to Margaret's word, all of Veronica's clients files were laid out with bullet points attached. Veronica checked her diary, and her first appointment wasn't until 10am. That was lucky, two hours to refresh her memory.

After her first appointment had finished, she had a window of thirty minutes in which she planned to make a phone call.

Veronica replaced the receiver with disappointment written across her face. Her final task for her Mother couldn't take place now until Tuesday week.

The weekend at Caroline and David's was a restful and enjoyable break for Veronica and Edward. On the Saturday afternoon the men went and played a round of golf at David's golf club.

Once the men had left, Caroline and Veronica sat in the garden with a pot of freshly made coffee. From the tray, Caroline picked up an envelope which she passed to Veronica.

"Veronica, this is Evelyn's letter, I would like you to read it".
Veronica took the proffered envelope and withdrew the sheet of writing paper inside. She read the note;

19th June 1978

My Dearest Caroline,
How well you have turned your life around. I could see how much love there is in your family and I am genuinely so pleased for you. You truly deserve it. Any Mother wanting the best for their child must be commended. My only regret, is that I never looked for you sooner. For Verity to be laid to rest with her rightful surname and the posies is more than you ever promised to do. Please accept this gift with the affection that it has been given.
I wish you and your family health and happiness,
Your friend
Evelynx

Veronica folded the sheet of paper and returned it to the envelope. She handed it back to Caroline. While wiping a tear from her face, she said,

"I knew she genuinely wanted you to have the ring. Now you can wear it, and please don't feel guilty in anyway".
A thought then crossed Veronica's mind,
"You do like the ring? Because if not I am sure it could be remodelled".
"Veronica I love the ring. That's why I felt so bad that it had been left to me. It is so beautiful".
"Then wear it and enjoy it. It would not only make Mum happy, but me as well".

That evening, Caroline and Veronica went by taxi to David's golf club, where they met their husbands for dinner in the restaurant. The following morning, they were introduced to Lady Sowersby-Smith, and she showed them around her new home. She was very keen to move in, and was happy to have the plastered walls just painted until it was possible to have them papered.
Caroline cooked them a delicious Sunday lunch, where they were joined by Andrea and Caroline's Mother. After tea in the conservatory, Veronica and Edward said their goodbyes.
Driving home, Veronica felt very contented. Edward glanced at her and thought she hadn't looked so relaxed for a while.
"Well Darling, I haven't seen you look so lovely in ages. You look so calm. We should get away

more often, although they are the perfect hosts, such a lovely couple".

"Couldn't agree more. Edward, while you and David were playing golf, Caroline showed me the letter Mum had left for her. Mum wrote that she wished she had taken the initiative sooner to find Caroline. How happy she was that she had made a success of her life. She also mentioned the posies that Caroline would place on Verity's grave, one on behalf of David and Sylvia and that she had managed to let Verity be laid to rest with her rightful surname. It was such a lovely letter that while I was reading it, it made me cry".

Edward touched her arm in acknowledgment. Veronica carried on.

"What is more, because Caroline is going to wear Mother's ring, they also agreed that Andrea should know the full story. They told her the day after the funeral, and do you know what Andrea said?"

Edward laughed,

"I haven't a clue, tell me".

"She said could they tell Granny, because Andrea thinks she has already guessed, and it would be kind to her to let her know that she was right, especially as she is getting old. So they have done, and Andrea was absolutely right! Lady Sowersby-Smith had known. From first meeting Andrea, she always thought she was her true Granddaughter. Apparently

Caroline's Father had his suspicions too but thought it would be best not to say anything. His belief was ignorance is bliss".

"My belief Darling, is as I have always said 'honesty is the best policy' ".

" Well" Veronica said. "It certainly has paid off this time".

Chapter Thirty Two

Tuesday week couldn't come quick enough for Veronica, another early start at the office.
Today she had a mission, and it meant leaving the office at 3pm.
By five past three Veronica was in her car. Her handbag and the jewellery box and envelope were on the passenger seat.
With- in fifteen minutes, she had parked her car and was walking into the entrance. It was with sadness now that she walked down the corridor, so much had happened since she had last been here.
She walked through the door and approached the small office. She tapped on the door and a voice answered.
"Come in, Hello Mrs Cousins, please take a seat. It's sad that we meet again in these circumstances and we were all very sad to hear about your Mother".
"Thank you Sister McDowell, that is very kind of you".
"Now, as you requested the young lady you wished to speak to doesn't know of your visit, so I will just inform her that you are here and then I will leave you alone".

"That's very kind of you Sister McDowell, thank-you".

Veronica sat waiting, and quite quickly, Sister McDowell returned with a very hesitant Staff Nurse Brown. Veronica had been hoping that there was somewhere she could go with Nurse Brown, somewhere more private. When Sister McDowell spoke it was quite clear that she wanted to be at hand.

"Mrs Cousins, I shall leave you here with Staff Nurse Brown, please take as long as you like". With that, she left the office and closed the door behind. Veronica could see that Nurse Brown was looking distinctly worried so she beckoned her to sit down, and then started her rehearsed speech.

"Nurse Brown, actually may I call you by your first name, mine is Veronica, it would make me feel more relaxed".

"It's Susannah".

"That's a lovely name. Well I am here today because my Mother left me some instructions to deliver a package and an envelope to you. I have no idea what is in either, so here they are. If you wish to open them in private then I totally understand, it is entirely up to you".

Susannah was still concerned with what they may contain. Had Mrs Compton planned some kind of unfunny joke? Susannah decided that she would open them in front of Veronica. She decided to open the package first. Evelyn had

sealed the jewellers box down with sellotape.
She gently removed the tape and flipped up the
lid to the box. She let out a gasp and turned the
box to show Veronica. Inside was a silver nurses
belt buckle, and resting next to it looked like a
silver nurses watch. Susannah lifted the watch
out, and then realised that the metal was not
silver but white gold. The watch had a beautiful
mother of Pearl face. She turned to Veronica.
"I don't know what to say? I don't think I can
accept these. The watch is obviously worth a lot
of money, and her belt buckles must have a lot
of sentimental value. It is really kind but I think
as her daughter you should keep them". She
handed the box back to Veronica.
"Why don't you read the letter I am sure it will
make things a lot clearer for you".
Susannah did as she was bade and opened the
envelope. She read:

19th June 1978

Dear Nurse Brown

I am sorry to be so formal but I don't know your Christian name, only that it starts with an 'S'. Please except these tokens of my appreciation. Without your help in suggesting I speak with my daughter, a worry that I have carried around with me for eighteen years would not have been resolved. The fact that you are reading this means that I have passed, and done so with a peaceful mind, which is attributed to you. I am eternally grateful.
With the kindness you showed me, my beloved watch and buckle have found the perfect home. Please wear them and I hope your career goes from strength to strength, you certainly deserve it,
Best wishes
Evelyn Compton

Susannah placed the letter on Sister McDowell's desk and then burst into tears. Veronica immediately reached into her handbag for a tissue for her.
Susannah started to wipe her eyes.
Veronica spoke in a very gentle voice.
"I did have a feeling that you may get upset. My Mother was a very kind and generous person, and I knew the letter would only be saying

complimentary things. As to you keeping them, there seems no doubt in my mind that they have found the right home. You truly did help her. Sorting out Mum's problem has opened up a new friendship in my life, which will help fill the void of losing her".

"I am so sorry Mrs Cousins I haven't even passed on my condolences. Your Mother confided in me because I had heard what she had been calling out. I knew by her voice that it had been something traumatic for her. Thank you for passing on this beautiful watch and buckle, I will always treasure them and thank you for reassuring me that everything has been sorted out. Now I can put to bed those words",

"What have I done, Oh no, what have I done?"

Afterword

My story evolved from a 'what if scenario'. The characters and places are all fictional. The idea came to me a number of years ago and only when I was recovering from surgery at the beginning of 2020 and then the country being put into a lockdown did I seriously sit and write. There by using my daily walks to work out the next bit of the plot.

Printed in Great Britain
by Amazon

40074035R00126